Heaven on Earth

VIOLA TEMPEST

Heaven on Earth

© Copyright 2022 Viola Tempest

All rights reserved.

No part of this publication may be reproduced, distributed, or transmitted in any form or by any means, including photocopying, recording, or other electronic or mechanical methods, without the prior written permission of the publisher, except in the case of brief quotations embodied in critical reviews and certain other non-commercial uses permitted by copyright law.

Any references to historical events, real people, or real places are used fictitiously. Names, characters, and places are products of the author's imagination.

Cover Design by Adrijana Cernic

CONTENTS

HEAVEN ON EARTH

VIOLA TEMPEST

PROLOGUE

Earth. They say God created the humans for a greater good, to allow them the freedom to make the best decisions that would benefit the creations of God, that would allow the Earth to prosper, just like God had intended.

The trees were created to allow these humans to stay warm, to build shelter. The oceans were created to help sustain life, to ensure that the humans would never perish from thirst. Crops and fruits were sprouted to keep these humans alive, to suppress their hunger, and keep them satisfied for another day.

But what God failed to realize, was that these

humans were flawed. A darkness had seeped inside them from Lucifer himself, causing these humans to turn evil, feral, and vicious. The freedom to make their own decisions and to do as they wished were not without repercussions. With darkness, came destruction, and soon, God's greatest creation began terrorizing everything he had constructed from his own heart and soul. From murder to cannibalism, the humans refused to stop.

It had started off so innocent at first, a few minor violations and crimes here and there. But as soon as the humans found out that they could get away with even worse, they took advantage of it, first by killing criminals and enemies, and then their families and friends, basically anyone who looked at them weird or rubbed them the wrong way.

And as time went on, God's trust in his humans began to fade, watching in horror and disappointment as his once pride and joy turned to the side of Satan, joining Lucifer's mission in his conquest to take down God and all things good. As a result, God decided to punish these humans, to wipe them all out and start afresh with a new batch who weren't tainted and manipulated.

And thus, an apocalypse was formed, turning all corners of the Earth into complete darkness, shadows looming above the heads of his people, and leaving nothing but evil in its place for the humans to finish each other off. The killings grew, with no regard for conscience or humanity. In fact, God even encouraged it, raining down weapons of mass destruction so they could shed blood in an ultimate massacre, and he could be done with them for good.

And so, the bloodbath continued over the next seven days. One by one, the humans fell to their very deaths. Escape seemed impossible, and everyone ripped each other into shreds until there were none left.

And on day seven, God could finally wipe out the Earth forever and never look back on his horrible mistake.

~ Lily ~

"Imalia! Imalia! Where are you?" Lily Caldwell ran down the streets of San Francisco, screaming out her sister's name.

They'd been inseparable, ever since they were just five years old. But since the start of the apocalypse, the city had been trampled by the hundreds of thousands of people either running for their lives or chasing to create chaos.

Lily and Imalia were just outside their shared apartment at Bodega Heights, when they heard a loud noise outside, almost like a gunshot, followed by shrieking screams and a horde of civilians charging their way. Imalia barely had time to push her sister aside before getting trampled herself, falling victim to the rush of the crowd and allowing herself to be taken away.

Oh, Imalia, if only she hadn't been such a caring big sister. If only they had stayed inside, barricaded with a bottle of wine and a rifle for protection. If only they had stayed in their tiny hometown of Van Dyne, Wisconsin, where their parents still lived, instead of having such big dreams to move to a major city. So many scenarios ran through Lily's head as she continued searching around all of Imalia's favorite spots, from the frozen yogurt stop she'd been obsessed with ever since they moved there, to the park they'd used to hang out in and laugh at the joggers who went by.

Lily sighed. Those were the moments. The good times. Oh, what she wouldn't give to revisit them all again.

But just her luck, everywhere she looked, even the subway station that Imalia swore she'd never step foot in even if her life depended on it, was empty. Well, not completely empty. Rotting bodies and stiff corpses covered the tiled ground like it was stitching together a sort of carpet, and Lily knew there was a 99% chance that her sister wouldn't be down there, but it was worth a shot.

Maybe she's hiding down here until the worst of it is over.

Lily shook her head. Even she couldn't make herself believe the nonsense that was spilling from her brain. Not like things could get any worse for the city of San Francisco. This *was* the worst of it. Sure, she'd seen druggies shooting up and crack heads shitting on streets, but those were nothing compared to this... this... mayhem of mass destruction.

Lily had always thought it'd be fun to live through an apocalypse, though the video games she'd played were a far more glorified version of the nightmare she was living in now. If only she'd kept her stupid wish to herself, maybe she wouldn't be stepping through human filth right now.

"Imalia! Imalia!" she cried out again, but the only sounds that reverberated were her own echoes. "Imalia, are you in here? Imalia?" she cried out again, tripping over a human arm that had snapped from its body against her foot. "Son of a bitch..."

She'd only been down here once, and only for a brief second. When she and Imalia first moved to The Golden City, Lily had all the intentions of riding the subway to work every day. Afterall, owning a car in such a populated city was the equivalent of throwing an entire bank account straight down the toilet. A simple train ride would've only taken her twenty minutes a day, not the forty that it ended up taking when Imalia insisted they chip in for a car.

Lily sighed again. She used to hate her sister, with her spoiled attitude and always getting her way. Ever since they were kids, Imalia always got her way, from the toys they received for Christmas to the guys she dated.

Ugh, not a dull moment went by where she didn't piss Lily off. But now, now in this apocalyptic shithole of a city, she'd give anything to have her back. She was the only thing left from her previous life, the only thread of normalcy she could hang on to, and the one thing keeping her moving forward. Her one motivation to survive this mayhem.

"Maybe this *is* karma," Lily whispered as she continued roaming through the subway. The escalator was out of service, forcing her to walk down a death trap of a machine that would swallow her whole at any minute. "Maybe all those years of wishing she were dead... I finally got my wish."

If she thought the sight of the underground station was bad, it wasn't nearly as bad as it smelled, like a truckload of nuclear waste had been dumped on top of a toxic dump in the most polluted ocean in the world. She tried her best to hold it all in, hold in the bile slowly rising up her throat, but the stench was just too overwhelming and what little remained of her lunch came back up anyway.

She took a second to compose herself, and then kept moving. Kept moving because it was the only thing she knew how to do.

The tracks of the station weren't much better than the platforms, the druggies once begging on the streets now decomposing where the rats used to search for crumbs. Now, they simply fed on the bodies themselves.

Nope, still nothing, not a single trace of movement from a human body. Not a single reply from her sister nor anyone else. Nothing but the quiet squeaks of the rats, and the silent whistling of the wind through the tunnel.

"Hello? Hello? Anyone here? Hello?" she called out, hoping that she'd find someone if she were in a different location, almost like the people were signals.

Suddenly, a hand grabbed her by the ankle. She flinched and looked down. The arm attached to the rotting hand was nearly detached from the body it used to belong to. Just one little... kick, and the arm came flying off and onto the tracks of train sixteen. When she glanced back down, the body had stopped moving, lying still with the rest of them.

Fear began stirring up in Lily. The city was usually dangerous enough when it wasn't going through an apocalypse. Now, there was a high chance of someone jumping out and stabbing her in the throat, killing her before she even realized it. And with no remorse, too. Killing for the sake of killing, and that was it. She often wondered why she was out there instead of hiding, instead of barricading herself and trying to ride the apocalypse out... But that wasn't like her. No. She'd promised Imalia that if they ever got separated, she'd go after her... and Lily had never broken a promise before.

I'll find you.

It felt like yesterday when she had said that. But she would; she would find her.

BOOM!

Lily heard gunfire from up on the streets, followed by screams from two, maybe three, people — one woman, two men. Lily could hear the rattling of footsteps as they charged down the street, in hopes of escaping whoever was after them. But soon, the screaming stopped, right after the sound of another gunshot.

Guess they didn't make it very far.

"Where next, boss?" One of the men asked another.

Lily didn't know just how many were up there, but if it was anything more than zero, she was in trouble. There were at least two standing up there on the street, maybe more, and she prayed that they didn't come down.

Sure, she'd taken a self-defense class before, but her one month of training definitely wouldn't be able to withstand whatever guns the men seemed to have up there. So far, she'd been just surviving, but with a whole lot of luck and will, hiding here and there, and avoiding danger like a madman dodging bullets.

"The subway," another man responded.

Probably the one in charge.

"On it, sir. We'll check every inch down there, and shoot anything that moves. No survivors!"

"No survivors!" Several others cheered.

Sweat began to pour profusely down her neck as she heard the clomps of their footsteps coming closer, first through the entrance, and then hurriedly down the stairs.

They were coming for her; she knew it. And they were going to find her and kill her. She quickly looked around. Nowhere to hide. She could attempt to hop onto a track and make a run for it down the tunnel, but the noise would give away her position. Plus, she was never one to be quick on her feet, constantly tripping over them instead. She could duck behind one of the many trash cans, even hide in one, but that'd probably be one of the first things they checked. There was only one thing for her to do, and it wasn't going to be pretty.

Less than a minute later, the men arrived. There were five of them in total, each carrying a large rifle and wearing spiked boots that she barely saw through her squinted eyes.

"Search every inch of the place. No survivors!" One man yelled.

The others all agreed in unison and spread out, a few knocking over trash cans while the rest hopped down onto the tracks of the tunnel.

Thank God, I screened out those options, Lily thought.

She could hear the men yelling, shooting their bullets haphazardly without a clear target, laughing as if they'd gone crazy with power. Lily waited a few moments longer. She'd wait as long as necessary if she had to.

"I got nothing, boss. You guys?" All the men regrouped nearby, the sound of clomping footsteps nearing her location. Too close.

"Nah, ain't nobody here. Let's bounce. These bodies are starting to really stink."

"Yeah, let's get outta here."

Lily continued to hold her breath and wish for the best. The stench from the rotting bodies was beginning to make her feel queasy, and she knew she didn't have much longer until she heaved out bile, her stomach too empty to let anything else out.

But still, it was either die by lack of oxygen or die by the hands of miscreants who were out for blood. Her blood. Whoever they were, she was sure they'd murder her if they found her, or at least, take her as their own to act as their personal slave.

The sound of footsteps started to fade, the men eventually climbing back up the stairs. Silence filled the subway again. Not even the squeaks of rats echoed inside the concrete walls when Lily finally knew it was safe to come out.

Pushing aside the stiff body of the man she had just torn the arm off of, she pushed herself through several others, who were all beginning to enter rigor mortis, holding her breath and brushing the pieces of human flesh off from her. It had been a good decision, too, in her mind. The rotting corpses definitely helped mask the smell of her perfume, which could have given her away.

Her life was spared... for now.

"Hiding from the Jaguars, too?"

She jumped at the sound of the deep voice.

"Who's... who's there?" she asked.

But when she looked around, there was no one to be found. Well, except for the corpses, but those didn't count.

"Who's there?" she asked again.

When she turned around once more, she saw a man around her age appearing from the shadows toward the left wing of the subway. He had jet black hair, shoulder length, and his eyes were even darker than his hair, if that was even possible.

He had a look of mystery on his face, like he'd experienced things, hardships, pain, like he had a story he needed to tell but was too broken to get it out. His leather jacket had a tear in the right sleeve, like he'd just gotten in a fight, and she couldn't tell whether the stains on his dark blue jeans were stains of blood or sewage water, or some kind of other fluid she'd rather not think about.

And she loved it, the way the tight denim wrapped around his tall, lean legs, and the way his biceps seemed to protrude from the thick leather. She didn't think it was possible for someone to look so threatening, yet so sexy, at the same time. And it'd been a while since she'd seen someone who didn't look at her like she was a body to add to a kill-count.

Oddly enough, she didn't feel personally threatened... Still, the fear of death caused Lily's body to tremble uncontrollably as he approached closer to her, and she backed away. He was clearly trying to look harmless, his hands free of anything sharp or penetrating, and stretched to his sides, palms up, and his smile more welcoming than menacing. But that didn't mean he couldn't pull a dagger out from behind his back, after all.

The city of San Francisco had become a true bloodbath, complete anarchy, no rules, no laws, utter chaos. Everything was free game now, including murder, and the city had truly become every man for himself. She didn't know how the rest of the country looked, how the rest of the world looked, whether it still functioned in an orderly manner or had gone completely radical. Either way, she had to find her sister, so together, they could figure out what was going on, figure out if there was still hope to get help and live a normal life again, or whether she'd be spending the short amount of time she had left running from the radicals.

"Name's Sydal," the man spoke up again when he came just mere inches away from her face. "Thought I was the only survivor left aside from the Jaguars. How'd you escape them, anyway?"

"The Jaguars?" Lily asked.

"Yeah, the Jaguars. Those morons who were just down here blowing up the place? It's what they call themselves, killing every last living being in the city of San Francisco, so they can claim it as their own and call themselves 'kings.' It's pretty absurd, really. What's the point of ruling if there's no one left to rule?"

"Oh, them, right. I hid under some of those bodies." She pointed to the stacked pile behind her. "Guess they mistook me for one of them, and stepped right over me. Lucky, I guess." She scratched the back of her head, tearing off pieces of the remaining debris from in between strands of her hair. "How do you know so much about them?"

Sydal shrugged. "Let's just say, I stumbled down the wrong alley at the wrong time. Found them taking down a nerd with a backpack. No mercy." He shrugged again. "But, then again, what's the harm, really, if it's the end of the world? No consequences. No rules. Everybody's just killing each other. And there's always one, too, in an apocalypse... One group who manages to make an apocalypse even worse by speeding it up." He scoffed. "As if people didn't have enough already to worry about."

"Do you know them? How'd you get away?"

Lily tucked a strand of her hair behind her ear and got closer, nerves rattling her frame, and the urge to know more pushing her forward. From there, she could see the thin jade ring around each of his irises, something she'd never seen on a human before.

Odd, she thought.

But she had more important things to worry about, like how the hell she was going to find Imalia, how she was going to continue outrunning these radicals who would find her soon enough, and whether Sydal, the handsome stranger standing before her, was someone she could trust, even if it didn't seem like there was anyone else here that she could turn to, instead.

"Morningstar," Sydal replied.

"Pardon?"

"Morningstar, my last name. Means bright planet. My mother always told me that's why I'm so smart, bright, like a planet. It's how I was able to hide from the Jaguars."

"I don't get it. You became a planet and hid in space?"

Sydal let out a belting laugh. "Ha! Funny. Nah, it was just a metaphor. Used my brains." He winked. "It also doesn't hurt that I know this subway inside and out. Been here many times to get to work. Here, come here."

He grabbed her by the right forearm and led her over to where he had emerged from earlier. That corner of the room was much darker than the one she had been roaming around in, but the smell wasn't much better. Blood stained the walls, and the stench of urine was noticeably coming from behind him.

"Ugh. What is it? I think I'm going to puke."

She lifted her shirt up slightly to covered her nose. But unfortunately, she was still able to smell the stink through her mouth.

"Just… around this corner." He led her around to the other side of a pillar and pointed up. "See that wooden plank up there?"

Lily looked up to where his finger ended. There was indeed a wooden plank nailed just a couple feet above her. No way could he have perched up there. There was barely enough room for the rats!

"It leads to an upper deck of the subway," he continued. "I slept up there once, or several times, before. The rent's just way too high in this damn city."

He was a strange one, for sure. Lily couldn't tell whether he was telling the truth or not, but what he was saying seemed too insignificant and meaningless to lie about.

Sleeping in the subway? Who does that?

"Yeah, it is," she replied. "I share a place with my sister, Imalia. Well…," she paused, "I used to, anyway. I'd be willing to pay the entire bill myself if it meant seeing her face again." She fell silent for a moment, then perked her head back up. "You haven't seen her, have you? Purple hair, my height, dressed in all black?"

Sydal shook his head. "Nah, you're the only person I've seen today. Well, unless you consider those monsters out there humans... which I don't. My best guess, she's either dead, or the Jaguars have her. Sorry to say this... uh, what'd you say your name was again?"

She shook her head. "I didn't. Lily. Lily Caldwell."

"Ah, pretty name. Anyway, Lily Caldwell, sorry to say this, but I think it'll take a miracle to find your sister, especially now. Whoever's still alive... I'm sure they won't be soon enough."

"No!"

"No?"

"No! I'm not giving up. And I'm definitely not going to stand here and listen to some stranger tell me otherwise. Get out of my way." She pushed her way past Sydal. "I'm going to find her."

She managed to make it halfway up the stairs before he called out to her.

"Wait!"

Lily turned around and saw the man skipping gracefully up the steps, almost like some ethereal creature.

"Wait," he repeated. "Let me come with you. I'll help you look. It's not safe out there alone. The Jaguars, if they find you, they'll kill you... or worse."

"What's worse than death?"

Sydal shook his head. "Torture, pure torture. Probably some other stuff that I don't even want to know. I'll help you. We'll stick together. Survival in numbers, right?"

Lily hesitated for a minute. Her instincts automatically told her not to trust him. After all, her mother always warned her about trusting strangers, telling her to be cautious when it came to the charming tricks of men. And she'd been good about it her whole life. But then again, this was different. She was literally in the middle of an apocalypse. If she didn't trust a stranger, there was no left she *could* trust. And they had spent a few minutes together, and she was still alive, right? If he wanted her dead, he would have done it already.

There was also something about him, an aura surrounding him that yielded a rope he had tied around her waist, pulling her closer and closer to him, even as she tried to continue up the steps.

Who is he? she thought. *And what does he want with me?*

But she couldn't think about that now; her sister was her priority. Imalia. And she had to find her no matter what, even if it meant enlisting the help of someone she'd met beside blood stains and dead bodies. She had no other choice.

"Okay." She eventually nodded. "Let's stick together."

CHAPTER
TWO

~ Heaven ~

Heaven looked down from where he perched atop his home's throne in the City of God. The sky was clear, but surrounded by dark and ominous clouds that overlooked the apocalyptic city of San Francisco.

Seven days ago, God had rained his wrath of embers onto his greatest mistake, the humans, the ones who brutally took advantage of the gifts he'd given them and turned them against him. He gave them a chance, a chance to build and grow as a society, but with all that power and freedom, came mass destruction and the seven deadly sins.

Such a shame, too. The human's Earth was supposed to be his greatest feat, a world where people were able to rise from a single ball of dough and mold themselves to become whoever they wanted to be.

And they did, to their own expense. Murdering each other and living a life of narcissism and big egos. Even when they're beginning to reach their own demise, the end of their mere existence, they continue killing, taking what they believe belongs to them rather than working together for a greater good.

It was a test, at first, a test to see whether they were able to come together and conquer during the greatest time of need. But no, slaughter and crime just got much, much worse, and by day seven, the human's Earth was barely in existence.

The angels didn't care. Neither did the saints, the souls, nor the venerated ancestors. They celebrated and danced to the songs of cherubs as they ate heartily and drank merrily at the fall of the humans. They knew there would never be a chance for them to conquer their own demons. They were too stupid, naïve, fragile, bound to fall victim to themselves.

And it didn't matter to the heavenly beings, anyway. Once the humans were wiped out, God would simply build a new world. With a different colony of humans? Maybe. Or maybe, with a different race entirely. Either way, it wasn't a concern for them. They could sit back, sip the finest of wines, and watch as the world below them burned into ashes.

Heaven scoffed at the insensitivity of the other angels. So pathetic. Relishing in the suffering of others? Sickening. All the humans were dropping like flies down there, either by the hands of their own kind, or from ever-burning flames that God had left on their soiled planet.

But he couldn't care. Heaven scoffed again and rolled his eyes. They deserved it, anyway. It wasn't like he didn't try to warn them. Ten days ago, he'd tried. He'd walked through the Golden Gates and disguised himself as a human being, his sworn goal to bring salvation to the humans and help them repent for their sins. He tried to warn them, tried to preach the word of God and what they needed to do to save themselves... but they didn't listen. They never listen and, because of that, they all deserved to pay for the consequences.

But still, his visit to the abyss down below hadn't been a complete waste of time. No, not at all. *Because of her*. Heaven had never felt love before in his life. In fact, he wasn't entirely sure what love even was. Were angels even capable of something so... so... emotional? But regardless of whether he could, he did.

Ah, he remembered it well. Trudging down the streets of San Francisco after being told off for the hundredth time, grumbling to himself that the planet was now doomed, and then he bumped into her, the most beautiful and magnificent specimen he had ever laid eyes on. Her glowing chestnut hair and sparkling blue eyes had captivated him, and he'd struggled to pull himself away.

"Sorry," she'd said.

He smiled at her, tugging at his brain to find the right words.

"You're magnificent!" he'd finally said, instantly blushing. "I apologize. Deeply. What I meant to say was, it's my fault. I should've paid more attention to where I was heading. Apologies again."

She giggled. "You're cute."

"Am I?"

The human nodded. "Especially when your cheeks turn red like that."

Quickly turning away, Heaven placed his fingers to his cheeks. Emotions weren't usually something that angels dealt with, though, humiliation was as common as having wings. But for some reason, he didn't feel cold nor indifferent toward the human standing in front of him. It was as if she had a magnetic pull on him, pulling him closer and closer to her.

Distraction crept up when he felt a hand on his shoulder.

"It's okay," she said. "I always blush around people I find attractive, too."

When Heaven spun back around, he noticed that

her cheeks were red also, the same as his, perhaps? No, it couldn't be. It was too perfect to be real.

"I'm Lily," the woman said then, extending a hand out toward him.

"Heaven," he replied without thinking.

"Your name is Heaven? How strange!"

He blushed again. He'd fucked up. He'd completely forgotten that he was supposed to be undercover. God had given him specific orders to never reveal his true identity while mingling among his creations. If any of them found out who he really was, the balance of the universe would shift, allowing his creations and all those evil a chance to walk through the Golden Gates, and this would put the keepers of the universe at risk.

Three angels. There were three angels who sat beside the throne of God and made sure the balance between the ethereal city and the creations below never got intertwined — except under dire circumstances.

Heaven used to be one of them, the lead guardian who watched over all the worlds of God's creations and made sure things never derailed from the plan. But that all had changed when he fell for the human, a compromise to his duty that got him dethroned from his position upon returning to God — and reassigned to act as the messenger between the voice of God and all his lowly creations, which included the humans.

"I mean... I mean... Heaven is my nickname. It's

what G... my mates call me, you know, because of my personality... and stuff. My real name is Hayden."

She gave him another look that made him feel like she was laughing at him. He'd never experienced mockery before, not a chance, a handsome and high-class stud like him. But he had seen the souls of those who had been on the losing end of his own mockery, and the look of pain he'd seen on their faces pained him. Right now, that's what he was experiencing.

"Hayden? Got a last name, Hayden? Or should I call you Hayden Heaven?" she asked, grinning from ear to ear.

Heaven laughed. The tension he had felt earlier during their conversation went away, and he started to relax around her, like he could stay with her forever.

"Maxwell," he eventually answered, pulling at strands of his brain for a name.

Angels were never assigned last names. They didn't have families, or ancestral history. To everyone in the City of God, he was simply just Heaven.

"Maxwell... I like that. Well, it's very nice to meet you, Hayden Maxwell. I'm Lily, Lily Caldwell."

Heaven smiled. *Lily, what a sweet name.* And someone he could definitely see in between his arms until the end of time.

Lily smiled back, her beautiful lips forming such a sensual curve that he wanted to reach out and touch them. "I have to go now, Hayden. My sister is waiting for me, but it was really nice meeting you."

Heaven watched as Lily turned around to walk away. He held his hand up and gave a tiny wave. He wanted nothing more than to chase after her, to get to know her better, but he knew he couldn't. He wasn't allowed to. The high council only approved his stay on Earth for a short while to try and save the humans. If they found out he was off chasing some girl instead, they'd surely revoke his privileges and send him back up.

"Hey, watch it!"

Heaven looked up and saw a man, carrying a cup and a briefcase, tilt over to the side while Lily lost her balance and started falling in the man's direction. Without thinking, Heaven rushed over and caught her just in time before her head collided with the ground. He didn't even stop to think about what others would think of his incredible speed, but they all clapped. It didn't matter, though, all Heaven could focus on was Lily, who threw her arms around him and gave him a kiss on the cheek.

"You saved me, Hayden! Thank you."

Heaven blushed again and slowly placed her on her feet. "My pleasure."

"Whoa!" Lily lost her balance again when she got on her feet. "I think I twisted my ankle or something."

"Can you walk?" Heaven asked.

"I think I should be fine; let me see..." Lily tried to take a step, and then fell over once again into Hayden's arms.

"Here, let me take you home." Heaven scooped up the human into his arms. "Just tell me where."

Heaven had walked the corners of many of God's created worlds before, each one much different than the last, some so much better than others. And the human world? It was definitely one fit for the bottom tier. The buildings were falling apart, and many of the human creatures looked miserable. God had given them all life, a place to call home. How could they possibly be so miserable? He didn't understand, but it wasn't his job to understand.

The human world was the only world he'd failed to fix. All the others either exemplified the gifts they'd been given by God or managed to turn themselves around. But the humans? They were all too stubborn to listen, too stubborn to understand that there was a greater power beyond them.

"Here we are!" Lily announced, still tucked safely in his arms. "Bodega Heights."

Heaven walked inside after Lily unlocked the door. It was nothing like what he was used to. The place was so cramped, so small, nothing like his own palace. Even the throne he usually sat on in his palace was larger than the entire apartment! Living in close prox-imity like this would drive him and all the other angels insane, but the human seemed perfectly content with such a small space.

"You can just drop me off on the couch," she said, pointing over to their left.

Heaven placed her down and gently touched the top of her head. "I hope you feel better soon, Lily Caldwell." But when he turned around to leave, she stopped him.

"Wait!" she called out. "You can stay if you like."

And tempting it was. Heaven turned back around and sat beside her. He was ahead of schedule, anyway. Surely, a couple hours on his own time wasn't going to do much damage.

And soon, those couple of hours turned into a couple of days. Heaven and Lily's relationship moved quickly, completely falling for each other later that same day and sharing a passionate kiss. Her lips were soft and sweet, and he wanted nothing more than to take her with him and save her. He didn't know whether she felt the same for him. Only God knew that, and Heaven certainly couldn't control how Lily felt.

But it didn't take long after they bonded before God summoned him back to where he belonged. His mission had failed. His work was done. There was no longer a need for his existence on Earth. And just like that, the woman he'd felt his first inkling of emotion for, the first person he'd ever fallen in love with, was out of his life, out of his reach. It tore his world apart, the way God used him as his little pawn for his bidding, just to take everything away from him when the deed was done. He deserved better than that. He deserved Lily.

Now, reminiscing back to his days on Earth only brought back painful memories. Sitting on his throne day and night, drinking away his tears, and watching the Earth burning down below.

But Lily was alright. And that was all that mattered. If he couldn't see her in person, the next best option was to watch her through the mirror that allowed him to look into all the different worlds in real time. It was the only option he had while he awaited for her to ascend. She had a good heart; he didn't doubt it. All he needed to do was wait for the apocalypse to fulfill its duty, and they'd be reunited once again. But even that felt like far too long of a wait sometimes.

Sure, the human world was quickly turning into dust, and the city of San Francisco, where Lily was, was overrun by corpses and sociopaths alike. But Lily was safe enough and content, not suffering, so that had to be enough for him.

Well, it wasn't exactly like God would allow him to go save her even if she wasn't safe. The fate of the humans was death, perish from the universe forever, and if any of the celestial beings interfered with that timeline, they'd be banished from the City of God forever. And Heaven didn't know anything else. He'd simply die if he was forced to live among the creatures created by God. It was too much to even think about.

"What's the point, even?" he muttered to himself as he took a swig from his bottle. "Nothing but creatures of their own destruction."

Then his gaze shot over to the mirror that kept tabs on Lily at all times, and his demeanor changed.

"Who in God's name is he?!"

Throwing his bottle against a marble pillar and shattering it, he sprung up from his throne and walked over to touch the surface, running a thumb over the brooding man's face.

"Sydal? Sounds sketchy. You better stay the fuck away from my girl."

~ Lily ~

"Come on, Lily," Imalia said. "What's the hold up? The movie's starting." Her tone was growing more and more agitated, but she had good reason to.

Friday nights were always their movie nights. It was tradition, ever since Lily was seven. Whoever got to pick the movie also had to prepare the snacks for the night and, this time, it was Lily's turn. A new movie called "The Eyes" had just been released on one of her streaming networks, and she'd been dying to see it all week.

It took days to convince Imalia to let her choose the movie again, because she'd already chosen the one last week. And that convincing came with agreeing to make an entire platter of appetizers, lined with potstickers, pigs in a blanket, eel sushi, and spring rolls. No, she didn't make it from scratch, not with her busy job of working at a law firm, but it took work stopping by several restaurants to pick everything up and organize them neatly all together on a plate.

"Coming!" Lily shouted back to her sister. The pressure was making her hands sweat and her body shake. She was never good with deadlines, which also made it difficult for her to be good at her job. "Ah, perfect." She stood back and admired her plating skills. "Super professional. Now, all I need is to pour the wine, and we're all set."

When she walked back into the living room with the platter, Imalia was flipping through channels; a bored look rested on her face.

"It's about time," she grumbled when she saw Lily walk in.

"Sorry, Imalia, it took longer than I thought to prepare everything. I hope you like — whoa!"

She tripped over the fold of the rug in the living room and lost her balance. And so did the platter, and everything flew into the air for a few milliseconds before they all came crashing back down onto the ground, the couch, and onto Imalia herself.

"LILY!!!" Imalia screeched as she peeled a potsticker off her hair. "Do you know how long I had to sit in the salon to get my hair done? Eight *fucking* hours! And now, it's all ruined!" Imalia pouted and stood up, wiping food off her clothes and hair. She was covered in all sorts of sauces and bits and pieces, even a drop of what looked like soy sauce running down her forehead. "Why don't you watch where you're going for once? It's always the same with you! You know, sometimes I think life would've been easier without a sister!"

Lily stood there in silence as Imalia stormed into the bathroom and slammed the door. It was an honest mistake, truly, but she didn't blame her sister. It wasn't like this was the first time something like this had happened. Lily *was* a klutz, always had been and always would be, and it didn't just drive Imalia nuts. Everyone who ever hung out with her knew this, and it was always a struggle trying to convince them to let her join in on their outings to bars or clubs. Even if she'd promise to be on her best behavior, it was never a promise she could uphold, and she knew that.

It was also the reason why she never had a steady boyfriend, always tripping over herself and embarrassing herself in front of hundreds of people at a time. People always got tired of her eventually, or she ruined things past the fixable point. And it wasn't only the physical part of her that was clumsy, she was also a mental klutz. She'd say things she didn't mean because she wasn't thinking, let secrets slip because she didn't think twice before speaking, and ruining all sorts of relationships because of this. It wasn't like she was a bad person; she didn't mean to mess up, but she seemed unable to help it.

She did find love once, however. Or, at least, she'd felt a love for him that she wasn't sure was reciprocated. Their relationship was short, just mere days, but there was something about Hayden that she could never seem to forget. He was sweet, gentle, like someone who wanted to dedicate his entire life to protecting her. They instantly connected when they met, and he'd laugh along and purposely trip on steps and sidewalks himself so she wouldn't feel so alone in her clumsiness.

He'd caught her and saved her from embarrassing herself when she tripped shortly after meeting him, and the way his hands felt on her back? She almost wanted to melt into his body. That's how she knew he was special, that she wanted him. It was in the way he looked at her, full of understanding and without any judgment. It was in the way he later listened to her, and how he gave her time to explain herself when she messed up instead of getting angry.

And when they kissed for the first time? Lily felt as

if her body was floating on a cloud, like the angels had lifted her into the skies of the Golden City and brought her to a place she never wanted to leave. Their whole time together had been magical, like something out of a movie. But, like all men, he had left her. Ghosted her.

One day, they were sitting on her couch, cuddling under some blankets and holding each other close, and the next, he had completely disappeared. No traces of a Hayden Maxwell ever existing. She looked for him everywhere, but no one had even heard of him. It was so strange, but she knew it was because of her. Her awkward behavior. Her clumsiness. Her inability to keep anyone around for long. He was just another stranger who had come into her life and left, despite how ethereal that experience felt.

But most of her clumsiness usually blended together, one moment of failure after another, too hard to keep track of. All except for one, one particular moment that she could never seem to get out of her mind... It was the day she met the woman. Maria, she'd said her name was. It was the only thing she had said, or the only thing Lily remembered. But she definitely didn't look like a Maria. More like a Delphyne or a Morgen. Something about her just seemed... evil, despite her normal appearance and even more normal way of speaking. And Lily couldn't look away.

The look that Maria gave her when they crossed paths, like she owned her or was trying to possess her, was all too much to handle. And the woman didn't speak; that was the strangest part. She just sort of stared at Lily, like she was observing her and studying her, looking her up and down and side to side. And then, before Lily realized it, a gust of wind jolted her body, thrusting her onto the ground and shaking the insides of her body. It had been a good day so far, not many clumsy mistakes, and then that had to happen.

And the weirdest of it all, when Lily looked back up, Maria was gone. She looked around trying to find her, and in her search, she realized that she had been the only one affected by the wind, the only one knocked over. The humiliation she felt then had no comparison to anything she had felt before.

I must've tripped, she thought to herself when she noticed several people staring at her. Classic, clumsy Lily.

"QUICK, OVER HERE!" Sydal loudly whispered and pulled at Lily's arm, leading her into a dark alleyway.

Memories of the past still danced in her mind, but the present was too harsh not to be pulled into it... everything around her completely in ruins, and her sister nowhere to be found. She'd give anything to get those moments back, to be able to finally sit on that couch with that platter of appetizers and just bond with her sister.

"What are we doing here?" she hissed back to Sydal.

"The Jaguars," he whispered. "They're on the hunt again."

He gestured for her to peer slightly behind the corner of the wall. From there, she saw at least five other men, all dressed in black and armed. Masks were covering their faces, making them unrecognizable, and their boots were covered in spikes that tore apart the bodies they each stepped over. One of them looked over in her direction, and Lily quickly pulled her head back.

"What are we going to do?! They'll kill us if they find us."

Sydal contemplated for a moment, and then pulled her further down the alley.

"Where are we going?" she whisper-yelled.

"The sewers. It leads to the East District. If we can make it over there unseen, there's a house we can hide in for the time being while we figure out our next move... It belonged to my grandmother."

"And what if they find us?"

Sydal shook his head. "They won't. There's a basement beneath the house that's impossible to locate unless you know what you're looking for... Granny was one of those people who thought a nuclear war was coming. And she had the means to prepare for it."

As Lily walked through the sewers moments later,

she could feel the dampness of the filthy water running into her shoes.

"Disgusting," she grumbled to herself.

Sydal chuckled. "I take it you're not used to this."

"By this, you mean trudging through the entire sewage system of San Francisco? Why, are you?"

He chuckled again. "Let's just say, I'm not exactly the model citizen around here. I've had my fair share of needing to outrun the cops."

She rolled her eyes. "Figures."

"Hey! If it wasn't for that, we might still be up there, outrunning the Jaguars in bright daylight. Is that really any better?"

"I guess you're right. At this point, I'll take what I can get. How far is this place, anyway?"

"Just a few miles, maybe three? But trust me, we'll be safe down here."

Suddenly, Lily stopped. "Are you sure about that?" She pushed a half-deteriorated skull with her foot. "Seems to me like we're not safe anywhere."

Sydal walked over beside her and grabbed her by the hand. "Don't worry, I'll keep you safe."

He smiled at her in a reassuring way and led her down the rest of the way.

Several hours later, or what seemed like it without any sense of time, they arrived at the house. It wasn't much to look at on the outside, a run-down home in a run-down neighborhood, but if it meant a chance at safety, Lily would walk into anything.

The interior of the home was a quintessential old person's home, with a paisley couch, a lace tablecloth, and more than several ornaments of cats lined up along the mantle of the fireplace. And there was certainly a distinguishable smell to the room, of dust, musk, and some sort of medical ointment. It wasn't something Lily had ever gotten used to, given that all her grandparents died before she was born.

"This way," Sydal called out.

She walked over and watched as he twisted a cat on the mantle, and the ground of the fireplace opened up. There was a set of stairs that led them down into a bomb shelter. As they quietly walked down, she could hear the echoes of their footsteps while she tried to maneuver around the cobwebs. It was beginning to become pretty obvious that this had been built a long time ago as a bomb shelter, but no one had been down there in a very long time — if not ever.

At the bottom of the stairs, there was another door that Sydal closed behind them, sealing them in, while Lily walked over to one of the cots and sat down. It wasn't nearly as cozy as her bed back home, but it sure beat sleeping on top of corpses. It didn't take long before Sydal walked over and sat beside her.

"So, tell me about this sister you're looking for... you two close?" he asked.

Lily shrugged. "I guess. We never really got along, but after we moved here from Wisconsin, we started relying on each other more as we didn't have anyone else." Lily sighed. "Truth is, I took her for granted most of the time, and I always resented her for being so perfect while I was the klutz."

"Nah, I think you're just being hard on yourself. Besides... I think you're perfect." Sydal shrugged like it wasn't a big thing, and Lily blushed deeply.

"Stop that, you don't even know me," she complained.

But secretly, she enjoyed his compliment. It wasn't very often that a handsome guy complimented her... or even looked at her.

"I know you well enough." He winked and then stretched his arms up. "What do you say we both take a nap? It's been a pretty rough day." He yawned and leaned back on his cot, crossing his legs at the ankles.

"Nap? Nap?! Are you serious?" Lily's blush turned into red anger. "The sun's still out, and I have to go find Imalia! I can't hide here all day and just... nap! I thought you had a plan!"

She could tell that she was growing unnecessarily hysterical, but she also couldn't control it. It had been a very stressful and long day indeed already, almost dying a few times and all.

"We'll look for her tomorrow, I promise," Sydal said, lifting his hands up in a surrendering gesture. "But right now, we're both exhausted, and the Jaguars are still out for blood. If we try to go up against them in this shape, there's no way we'd get away alive."

He had a point, and she knew that.

After trudging through that sewer, there was nothing more she wanted to do than sleep. But how could she sleep when she didn't know what was going on with Imalia? Where she even was? It was exhausting, this running, and surviving, and not knowing.

"What about other cities? States?" she asked after a few minutes of silence.

"What about them?"

"Do you think there are survivors? Civilization? Maybe San Francisco is the only place affected. Maybe Imalia is in Oakland, or Berkeley! Maybe she got out of town!"

Sydal only shook his head. "I doubt it. I've been to several towns myself looking for survivors... they're all the same. Destroyed and in ruins. I doubt you'll find many people who are still alive..."

The news settled into Lily's stomach like a heavy rock. All cities... all the same... Was there any hope left?

"But... but... but we still have to try! There might be other survivors in places you haven't looked... People who can help us? We can't be the only ones left!" Her hands were shaking by this point, her voice trembling, and tears threatening to fall from her eyes.

"Hey, hey, hey, Lily. It's okay. It's okay. Look, trust me, okay?" Sydal went over to her cot, sitting by her side and running a reassuring hand up and down her back. "Tomorrow, we'll go out and look for her. And if we can't find her in San Francisco, we'll branch out. City by city, scouring every town until we find her.

Okay? Just trust me and rest for a while, now that you can."

Lily nodded, tears now streaming down her face. She didn't have much faith in this stranger she had only just met, but there weren't many options left. If it wasn't for him, she may have ended up being the Jaguars' next victim.

He then leaned over and kissed her on the cheek, and when she didn't resist or protest, he turned her head slightly and planted his lips onto hers. It was soft and gentle, almost like a question. His lips tasted salty, but then she realized that it was from her own tears. Their kiss grew into something sensual and smooth, and she felt her body gravitating toward him with each dance of their tongues.

"You're so beautiful," he whispered as he tilted back slightly to speak.

And then he leaned over and kissed her again, harder this time.

She didn't complain, not one bit. Her failed dating experiences in the past danced in her mind, the irony that she'd find a fine and handsome man to ravish her like this on the brim of an apocalypse. Was this ideal? No, it wasn't, but her body was deprived of a man's touch, and her body demanded what her mind couldn't have.

She kissed him back, allowing his hands to fall down her back and around her waist. She knew she had to find Imalia, but right now, all she wanted to do was kiss Sydal, to feel the comfort he was providing. If this were her last days on Earth, she wanted someone to fall back to, someone who would protect her and help her in a way no one in her life had before, in the way Sydal had in the few hours they'd known each other.

CHAPTER
FOUR

~ Lily ~

The next day, Sydal failed to keep his promise.

"I need to rest my legs," he said when they were up in the morning. "I think I tore something yesterday... can we go tomorrow?"

He poured out some beans that were stored in the bunker, and kissed her again when she got upset. And tomorrow became tomorrow again, Sydal making excuse after excuse.

It was two weeks later when Lily finally had enough.

"That's it! I can't just keep sitting here! If you won't come with me, I'm going alone!"

She sprung up from the cot and stormed toward the door of the bunker, but Sydal held her back right before she reached the handle.

"Lily, please. It's not safe out there! Not yet. I know the Jaguars are hungry for survivors right now, and if they catch you, they won't show any mercy. I can sense it. I can sense that you'll be in great danger if you walk out there. Please, believe me."

Her scowl quickly turned into a sympathetic look when she saw how sincere he was being. He was practically begging her to stay, like he truly cared for her safety. But sense it? Really?

"No." She shook her head, breaking out of whatever trance-like state he had put her in. "I'm sorry, but I have to find her... I have to find Imalia. It's the only thing I can do to make things better," she whispered under her breath, talking only to herself.

She pulled out of Sydal's reach and lifted her hand to the knob, to get out, when suddenly, she found her head hitting the ground, her mind going blank, and everything around her turning black.

"Lily! Lily!" A voice called out to her insistently.

When Lily finally opened her eyes again, she was no longer inside that cramped bunker she had been living in for the past couple weeks. Instead, she found herself standing... on a cloud? She glanced down; the entire city of San Francisco was below her, in ruins.

She nearly lost her balance; she wasn't afraid of heights, but damn! Was this an illusion?

"Lily! Over here!" The voice called out again.

When Lily found where the voice was coming from, she walked over, to the Golden Gates. There, she saw a familiar face, one she felt like she'd seen before, but she couldn't quite put the face's name on her tongue.

"I know you," she said. "I've seen you before."

And she had. The man standing before her looked so much like the only man she'd ever truly loved, like Hayden Maxwell. But it couldn't be. This man was almost transparent, a halo levitating over his head... and his voice, his voice sounded unreal, almost god-like, ethereal. No, he couldn't be Hayden. Hayden was gone; he'd disappeared, probably either missing or dead because of the apocalypse.

The man blushed, yet another thing that Lily found strangely familiar.

"Hayden?" she asked dubiously, even knowing it couldn't be possible.

"My name is Heaven," he said. He had golden brown eyes, and the aura around him seemed to light up the sky. "I am your guardian angel, and I'm here to protect you."

Of course, it was too good to be true. She was delirious.

"Protect me? Protect me from what?" She found herself asking.

"Lily, Lily, wake up! Wake up!"

Lily opened her eyes again, finding herself back inside the bunker, lying on top of the cold, stiff cot. Sydal was sitting beside her, a hand resting on her arm as he shook her awake.

"What... what happened?" she asked.

"You had a nightmare. Mumbling in your sleep about cake or something. It was very odd. I thought I'd wake you up to see if you're okay."

"Thanks."

Lily thought nothing else of the dream when she ventured upstairs to look for a couple cans of soda. The bunker was well equipped with canned goods, enough to last an eternity, but there wasn't anything delicious or sugary there, and sometimes, she craved something different.

In fact, there wasn't much more there than cans, the same few things being eaten one day after the other. Sydal allowed her to go upstairs once in a while, but made her promise never to leave the house without his permission, lest she wanted to die. And for some reason, she trusted that he was only looking out for her, doing what he believed was best for her. After all, hadn't he saved her life?

Heaven, the name popped into her mind. *Such a strange name.*

She grabbed the sodas from the storage closet and headed back downstairs, tossing a can over to Sydal before popping one open herself.

"So," she began. "When are we going out to find Imalia? It's been weeks, and I'm worried something terrible is going to happen to her if we don't find her."

She hoped, most of the time, that Imalia had been as lucky as her. After all, *she* was the klutz, so if she had survived this long, she had to be confident that Imalia had, too.

"Soon enough," Sydal assured her, taking a sip from the can. "When the moment is right, I promise. I'm sure she's okay... From what you've told me, she's smart, feisty. She can fight off the Jaguars if it comes down to it, right?" He said almost noncommittally, like it was obvious that she would.

Lily had talked a lot about Imalia, sharing memories of her with Sydal almost daily.

"I don't know... I know I wouldn't be able to."

"Well, but she's tougher than you, right? And you have me for protection, so you don't need to fight for yourself. I'm sure Imalia can handle herself."

And with that, Lily let it go once again.

LATER THAT NIGHT, she found herself standing outside those same Golden Gates.

"It's good seeing you again, Lily," the man, Heaven, or whatever his name was, said again.

"How do you know my name?" she asked, walking over to him.

"I know everything." He smiled at her, his lips so beautifully placed as he turned them into an upside-down arch.

"Are you God?"

Heaven laughed, his head tilting back when he did. "No, but I am one of his right-hand men and, specifically, I'm in charge of overseeing the human world, your world, among other things."

She raised her right brow. "I don't believe you. In charge of the human world? Who exactly are you?"

"I'm your guardian angel."

And soon enough, Lily saw wings of glory extend from the man's back. They were the most beautiful things she had ever seen. The feathers were so surreal that she couldn't believe her eyes. Even for a dream, the man in front of her seemed so realistic, like she'd seen him in real life.

"Lily, Lily, wake up! Wake up!"

Lily opened her eyes and found Sydal sitting beside her once again, shaking her lightly.

What's happening to me?

Her head was pounding when she sat up, like a truck had rolled her over. This was the second time dreaming about that same world now. It couldn't be just a coincidence, could it? Why did she keep having these dreams? Who was Heaven, and what was he trying to tell her?

"Come on, we have to go," Sydal interrupted her

thoughts and threw a backpack at her before throwing one over his own shoulders.

Her head felt like it was about to split open with the pain she was feeling, and she was utterly confused as to what was going on. After weeks of being trapped inside, they were finally going, so urgently...

But going where?

~ Lily ~

"Where are we going? To find Imalia?" Lily asked hopefully as she rubbed at her temples, the headache growing worse with the sound of Sydal's footsteps as he walked toward the stairs.

"Not yet. Just a little bit longer for that... But we're running low on some supplies. We have to go out and find some. We have enough food to last us for days, but we're almost out of toiletries and medicine. If anything bad happens, and you injure yourself, I won't be able to help you."

"Maybe we'll get lucky and find Imalia in the process," Lily said, again hopefully, as she threw the bag over her shoulders and laced up her boots.

"Doubt it," Sydal muttered. "There's a high chance that she left town already, or is in hiding. She won't be lurking around shops. No point in anyone really wandering around these quarters if they don't have to."

"Maybe, but it's still worth a try. Not like we're losing anything... Maybe she's in need of supplies, just like we are"

Sydal only rolled his eyes, like he had lost complete interest in both her and her mission. Lily didn't understand why he was suddenly so cold toward her. Just days ago, he told her how beautiful she was, and how he wanted to be there for her no matter what. He had looked after her for days. And now, it seemed like he had lost complete interest in trying to help her find Imalia, in everything he had promised her when she agreed to join him at the beginning. It was like the previous weeks were a blur of facts that didn't make sense or add up in her mind. Had she imagined all his promises? Had they been a part of her dreams and nightmares?

Walking out of his grandmother's house felt like walking into a war-torn country. The East District had gotten much worse since they first arrived at the house, like someone had run a bulldozer through the entire neighborhood. The cars that used to sit on the streets were now jumbled into a massive pile of scrap metal. The homes that used to line up the sidewalk had all collapsed in on themselves, and bullet holes could be found in every direction she looked.

"Do you think they know we're here? Are they looking for me?" she asked Sydal, pulling her backpack closer to her body, her eyes nervously scanning their surroundings.

"Possibly," he replied, running his fingers along the newly formed holes on the pillars of his late grandmother's home. "Though, I'm not sure how they found us. They must have a dog."

Could they do that? Was that logical? She wasn't sure anything made sense anymore.

"Is it still safe to go? They might be waiting for us, ready to shoot as soon as we move."

"We don't really have a choice, Lily. If we want to stand any chance in defending ourselves against them, we need to be better armed. We need to find guns and ammo, too. Bulletproof vests... We need to arm ourselves."

Was that why they were going out? Lily didn't know what to say; she wasn't ready to die, and definitely not by the hands of other humans. Hell, she still hadn't found her sister. No way was she going to let it all end without doing what she sought out to do in the first place.

"I... I think we should just go back inside. It's not

safe out here," she whispered not even a block later as her body shook with fear.

She tried to turn around toward the house, but Sydal grabbed her before she could even take a few steps.

"Lily, wait! Don't be a fool. We *have* to go. There's no other choice. How do you expect to find your sister if you can't even go out to pick up a few supplies? If we don't go, we'll die. Come on, Lily... I can't do this without you," his tone softened with the last sentence, and he grabbed her by the arms, pulling her close to him and smacking his lips against hers.

Lily felt her body sinking into his arms, like butter melting against a hot pan. She didn't know why, but at that moment, all the woes and reserves she had about following Sydal into his death trap seemed to all vanish away, like she had become a puppet to his mastermind of manipulations. When he told her it would be okay, she had to believe him.

"Stop freaking out, okay? We'll be fine. We're only going down a couple streets."

Lily nodded. "Okay," she said, wiping the tears from her eyes, and taking Sydal's hand as he led her down the street.

She had never explored the East District before. When she and Imalia first arrived in San Francisco, everyone warned her against it, an area known for its crime and poverty. The Tenderloin, especially — that was always the worst. She'd never been, but she'd heard stories from coworkers who had either gotten mugged there or knew someone who had been the victim of violent crimes. The horror was always too much for her, scaring her away before she even had a chance to go near it.

"Have you lived in San Francisco your whole life?" she asked, breaking the silent tension between them and wanting her mind to stray away from the scary thoughts.

Sydal was staring straight ahead, his eyes focused on the road, one hand gripped tightly around the straps of the bag and the other still holding her.

"My entire life," he responded, still looking straight ahead. "My whole family grew up here, generation after generation. And I'd be damned if I let a group of imbeciles chase me out of my own hometown."

"I'm sorry," she whispered.

"For what?"

"For going on and on about finding my sister when you probably have family who are either missing or gone. I never even thought to ask whether you needed help. I'm sorry I'd been so selfish."

He just shrugged. "Don't sweat it. I've pretty much accepted that they're gone. I've given up hope of trying to find them. My only mission now is to survive, to show the Jaguars that they can never take the fight out of the Morningstars."

"I like that. True passion. I'm glad you're on my side." She squeezed his hand tight, smiling at him.

The rest of the journey remained in silence, but not for much longer. They soon arrived at a gas station, one smacked in the middle of the city that went from being extremely populous to looking like a tornado had ripped through it. Sydal stepped over a couple bodies and opened the door, which barely hung on to its hinges. He peered inside briefly before gesturing for her to follow him inside.

Lily took a deep breath, preparing herself for whatever smells or danger were waiting inside, and proceeded. *A literal ghost town!* She'd been in gas stations before, always heading inside to purchase the snacks while Imalia filled up their car. She'd normally expected fully stocked shelves, chips on the left, cakes on the right, and drinks lining up the back of the building. But in this case, she found herself staring at nothing but empty shelves, not even a single can of beans to be found.

She watched as Sydal ransacked the shelves, smashing his fists against a few when he discovered they were all bare. She tried looking under a few, in case something had fallen while the desperate were busy grabbing and hurrying to get out.

But no. Nothing.

She looked under another one, and far out of her reach, she spotted a small bag of rice. She went down on all fours and extended an arm out. So close, but her arm was just too short to reach.

"Hey, Sydal!" she called out.

"What is it? I'm busy trying to find something useful in this fucking store!"

He sounded agitated, and the last thing she wanted to do was bother him even more, but if he didn't help her, someone else might end up snatching this bag of rice.

"I found some food! Well, a bag of rice, but I need your help getting it. I can't reach it."

Still down on her hands and knees, she could hear his footsteps getting closer, paired with something that sounded like metal screeching against the floor. But she didn't think much of it, the shelves were all metal, and he had probably just hit one of them, scraping it against the floor.

"Where is it?" he asked.

Lily leaned under the shelf a little more. "Back there, toward the wall. Your arm is longer than mine; maybe you can reach it."

But instead of the nod of agreement and the bending down of his own knees to help her out, she heard the scraping of metal again.

"Sydal?" she asked, pulling her head out from beneath the shelf.

Before she could say another word, her vision turned black. She remembered seeing a glimpse of Sydal, a metal pipe in his hand as he stood over her. Had she seen him swipe the pipe toward her before her entire world turned dark? Was that part of the nightmare? Or the dream?

"Lily, Lily! Over here!"

She slowly opened her eyes. There were clouds below her feet, and the ruins of San Francisco down below. Heaven was calling her name through the Golden Gates.

And the pain. She vaguely remembered the pain she'd felt for a brief second after a blow to her head. Had it been a blow to her head? But now, it was gone, like she had magically healed herself, or like nothing had happened.

Regardless, she'd had enough, enough of dozing off into this strange world every time she passed out, enough of listening to some stranger shout out her name every time she tried to recover from whatever migraine she was experiencing. She stormed over to the gates and demanded, "Okay, I'm tired of this. What's going on? Why do I keep coming back here? I need to know what's happening to me!"

She expected the man to say something bizarre, that this was only her imagination, and whatever she was experiencing was nothing more than a figment of her own creation. But he didn't. What he said was worse.

"You're in danger," he answered. "That man down there with you, Sydal, he's up to no good. You need to find a way to escape, run far away from him before it's too late."

She scrunched her face and pouted. "What? That's insane! Sydal's a good man. He's protecting me from the Jaguars, and he promised to help me find my sister. Why would someone evil do that?"

"You don't understand," Heaven retorted. "I know what he's capable of. He's not trying to protect you. He's been following you, and he's been manipulating you into believing him so he can swoop in and destroy you when you least expect it."

That didn't make any sense.

"No, you don't understand. You don't know anything about him!"

"Then how do you explain running into him after seeing no one else around for so long? How do you explain the headaches and migraines you've been having when you wake up every time you black out? Why has he been putting off helping you week after week? How do you explain all that, Lily?"

"Stop! Stop it!" She threw her hands over her ears to drown out his voice, the headache creeping back in at the sound of her own screams. She refused to believe anything Heaven had to say. Sydal *was* protecting her. He was there for her when no one else was, and she'd be damned if she let some creature in her dream tell her otherwise.

"Lily! Listen to me, please! You have to believe me. You have to protect yourself!"

"Shut up! Shut up!" She continued to scream as loud as she could, shaking her head to try to get rid of the dream, but was soon interrupted by the feeling of cold water splashing against her face.

"Wake up, you're dreaming again!" Sydal's voice reached her.

Shaking the water away from her face, Lily slowly opened her eyes. She was starting to doubt what was real and what was part of her dreams. The last thing she remembered seeing before falling back on the clouds was Sydal standing over her with a metal pipe... much like what he was doing now, back in the bomb shelter.

"What... what's going on?" she asked. She then looked over at her wrists, the cold feeling of metal steering her attention to them. "Why am I in chains? Sydal, what the hell is going on?"

But Sydal only laughed — the vociferous laughter coming from the force of his belly shook the room around her, and she could feel herself standing in front of Death's door. It had been real, the metal pipe, the dream?

"Didn't your parents ever tell you not to trust strangers?" he asked in a conceited tone.

"*Who* are you?" Lily demanded.

He grinned at her, a look of evil washing over his features.

"I said, who are you?!" she yelled again.

His grin grew wider. "I think you already know."

Her mind flashed back to the day they first met. She'd been running up and down the streets of San Francisco, with absolutely no one else in sight for miles. But in only mere seconds of the Jaguars appearing and leaving, Sydal had appeared. She hadn't seen any other survivors before... No, it couldn't be.

"You're... You're one of them?"

Her voice was trembling. She still had so much to live for, so much she wanted to do, even in the midst of an apocalypse. And she'd trusted him, too, fell in love with him, gave herself to him. But he had been using her all along, and this... this charm he kept portraying was nothing but a lie. It was nothing but a way to trick her. But why? Why play with her like this?

Sydal nodded. "Yeah, yeah, I am. I'm actually surprised it took you this long to figure it out. How'd you think I knew so much about them? Climbing up a two by four to hide? It was such a ridiculous idea that I never thought you'd fall for it. But you did, and that only made it that much easier for me." He snorted. "Ah, such a stupid, stupid girl."

"What do you want with me?!"

As she shouted, she tried to pry her hands through the cuffs of the chain, but the more she pulled, the tighter the cuffs became. Soon, her hands started to turn both purple and red.

"You're a special girl, Lily. Do you know that?" he asked her.

She spat some blood onto the ground, a few particles splashing the cot. "I thought you said I'm stupid."

He let out another laugh. "See? Smart, I like that. But not too smart. You see, Lily, I've been following you for quite some time now, even before the apocalypse. You have something very special inside of you that I very much want."

"I refuse to have sex with you, not again!" she spat.

Sydal, if that was even his name, let out a horrible laugh, a sound that shouldn't have belonged on Earth.

"Ah, but that's where you're wrong, Lily. The thing I want isn't your body. Silly girl, again! It's your soul!" He laughed once more, his face getting closer to her. And then he said the one word that changed everything. "Maria... Does that name ring a bell?"

Maria, Lily thought. *That woman I bumped into, the one who wouldn't stop staring at me and gave me the creeps?*

"What are you talking about? What do you know about Maria?" she yelled out. "What do you want with me?"

"Oh, you'll find out soon enough. The ritual has yet to begin. You won't want to ruin the surprise now, do you?"

"I think I do if it gets me the fuck out of here!"

"Feisty, I like it. You keep surprising me! You'll see, patience *is* a virtue, after all." He leaned over and stroked her hair before she managed to tug herself away from his grasp. "Feisty, feisty. I like it," he repeated.

Then he straightened up and walked out the door.

Finding herself all alone, Lily felt hopeless, hopeless that she'd never find Imalia, and hopeless that she'd never make it out of there alive.

"I'm sorry, Imalia," she said, bowing her head. "I've failed you."

Hours passed by, and Sydal still didn't return.

"Probably out kidnapping more people," she quietly whispered to herself.

The night was growing dark, not like she could see outside, but her body was beginning to grow weak and tired, her eyes drifting shut.

"Hey, Lily."

Her head sprung up at the sound of the voice, and there, standing before her, was him. The man in the sky. Heaven. She looked around, expecting to find her body perched on a bed of clouds and away from the confines of Sydal and his horrible gang of minions. But no, she was still here, still cuffed in those metal chains that took away her humility, still trapped in that horrible dungeon Sydal had convinced her to go into.

She looked back up at Heaven, blinking several times before realizing that he wasn't going away.

"Hayden?" she asked dubiously.

CHAPTER
SIX

~ Heaven ~

Heaven took a long swig from his bottle and found himself incredibly lonely. He'd lived for centuries, and each one felt more like a life of solitude and celibacy than the last. He looked out his window — all the other angels were still partying their hearts out, dancing on top of the clouds and living a life of hedonism.

He sighed. He could have that, if he wanted. But he didn't. He never did. His entire existence, he'd been in search of one person, one person whom he felt like he could truly connect and form a bond with. But he could never find the one — not until it was too late, anyway. He'd been out with a few... well, many, but he always came home alone to an empty house after a night of meaningless fun.

The female angels always wanted him, looked for him — he was quite a looker, but he never wanted any of them, finding them too pedantic and superfluous. And until recently, he figured he'd just end up alone forever, live the life of a bachelor until the end of his time.

But then he met her, Lily Caldwell, the one woman who gave him one striking look and took his breath away. The one woman he'd ever fallen for, the one woman who reached into his body and stole his heart.

"Hey, Heaven, why the long face? Come outside and party with us. The dumb humans down there are all killing each other... I mean, they're practically doing the work for us."

Heaven turned his head from the window and saw Gabriel standing by the door, a glass of champagne in one hand and a platter of shrimps on the other. His hair was ruffled, and his left wing looked like it had seen better days.

"Not in the mood, Gabe." Heaven sighed heavily and turned his head back toward the window. "Besides, an entire world is crumbling right beneath us. How can you celebrate when so many people are dying?"

"Ha! You're such a fake! Come on, Heaven, I know you used to party the same as us before. What changed? Don't tell me it's all about that human? It's not like you care about the entire human world, anyway; you just care about her." Gabe popped a shrimp into his mouth, unconcerned, but Heaven's blood boiled at the comment.

"How'd you know about her?" Heaven's eyes perked at the comment, his body shifting off the throne as he took a step toward his friend.

"Really? You think after you were dethroned as God's right hand, I wouldn't know what happened? I was his left hand; now I have to be both... It's been exhausting, but rewarding." He popped another shrimp into his mouth. "It was actually quite amusing, you know, seeing you fail so hard... You used to be the better one between us; now I guess I am." He broke out into laughter, and Heaven's face grew hot.

Heaven and Gabriel had been close from the start, but with their relationship being as close as brothers, it always brought a lot of animosity and a sense of competition between them. And now, Gabriel was coming out on top again.

"Out! Get out, Gabe! And leave me alone!" He grabbed his bottle and threw it at him, missing Gabriel barely by an inch.

"Whoa! Whoa! Calm down!" Gabe glanced around, making sure the coast was clear before walking closer to Heaven. "Okay, what about this...

let's make it even... I know God was maybe a little bit hard on you, so what about I lend you a little hand? You can never tell anyone I told you this, but rumor has it, there's this cherub, Cael... he can help you get inside a creature's dream... a human's dream. Help you communicate with them, like they're standing there with you face-to-face."

Heaven stared at him for a few seconds before turning his head away. "I don't believe you. That's insane! No one can do that, not even us. Heck, I'm not even sure God has the power to do that."

"We don't! God, well... maybe. But it's worth a shot, right? With Cael's help, maybe you can talk to her again, see her again. With the flames rising and rising, there's no telling how much longer she may have left. I know God thinks you messed up, but brothers gotta stick together."

Heaven thought about rolling his eyes and brushing Gabriel aside. He was drunk. He didn't know what he was yammering about. Communicating through dreams? Everyone knew worlds couldn't cross like that without approval from the high council. It would distort the entire universal timeline!

But this loneliness... All the worrying... It was too unbearable. If there was a chance for him to speak with Lily again, he had to at least try, right? Even if this was all just a rumor, he had to find out. Otherwise, he'd be stuck mulling over the what ifs.

"Where can I find him?" he asked Gabriel, who was now licking his platter clean.

"Huh? Find who?"

"Cael, the cherub! Where can I find him?"

"Ah, yes, him. I believe he lives in a cave in the Whimsical Caves. You know, the ones beside the Enchanted River? It's where all the cherubs live."

"I know the one. Thanks." Heaven stood up from his throne.

"Wait! Don't you want to have a drink with us before you go? I hear Charmaine has had her eyes on you for quite some time. She *is* the finest of the fine," Gabriel shouted after him as Heaven approached the door. "Plus, these shrimps are FANTASTIC!"

"No, thanks. I have to find Cael. I'm running out of time."

He turned back around and walked out.

"Good luck! And if you get hungry, you know where I'll be!"

The Whimsical Caves were located in the far south of the City of God. The cherubs weren't the most respected; angels were usually held on higher thrones. But the cherubs were smart. They didn't care about what the rest of the Golden City thought because they knew their place, and they knew what they were capable of. Without them, the City of God may not have stayed afloat for as long as it did. The cherubs were equivalent to the elves of Santa's workshop.

As Heaven crossed the Enchanted River, he smiled as the frogs leapt in and out of the crystal-clear water.

"Hi, Heaven," one of them said. "Going to see the cherubs?"

Heaven nodded. "Hey, Hopscotch, yeah. I've never been down here before, but I'm here to see Cael."

"Ah, Cael," Hopscotch croaked. "You're not the first one to come down here for him. Trying to hack a dream, I see. Let me just tell you this: Cael, a very stubborn cherub, but he knows his stuff."

"Have you gone to him before?"

Hopscotch shook his head. "Nope, but I have seen many, and I mean many, other angels run by here in tears of both humiliation and joy after speaking with Cael. I have no doubt that you'll get what you're looking for. You might just cry a little, is all."

"Very funny. If this guy's really as good as they all say, I could care less if he makes me piss myself."

"Suit yourself. But don't say I didn't warn you."

With that, Heaven crossed the bridge to the quarters of Whimsical Caves. There were hundreds of individual caves stacked on top of one another, each one looking the same as the last... exactly the same. But still, it didn't take Heaven long before he found the one that belonged to Cael. The large fluorescent neon letters spelling out his name at the entrance certainly didn't do a great job of concealing his privacy.

Shaking his head, Heaven walked toward Cael's

cave, ignoring the dancing fairies circling around the front. He extended his wings, ready to fly up to the high cave entrance, only to find the strongest winds he'd ever encountered pushing him back down toward the rocks. He nearly lost a wing with the hard crash, and had to keep going by foot. The walk up the steep mountain was rough, getting on his hands and knees to climb his way up the rocky slope. He was never one to engage in exercise, or any type of labor, to be honest, but for a chance to see Lily, he knew it'd be worth it.

A few scratches later, he finally made it to the front door. By then, his wing was healed again, but he was exhausted, so Heaven sat down and leaned his back against the exterior of the cave while he healed his other wounds and caught his breath.

"This better be worth it," he muttered as he proceeded to knock on the rainbow-colored door.

"Knock, knock, knock, race against the clock!" Heaven heard a jolly voice say from the other side of the door.

A few seconds later, the metal door swung open, and a short, stubby cherub, with glistening pink wings and a rose tucked behind his ear, floated out. He had a wide smile on his face, but a judgmental stare in his eyes. Heaven didn't know whether to smile back or run away. The look he was giving him was just so daunting.

"You, I know you. Heaven, the man who practically

destroyed Earth because he couldn't save them in time."

Heaven's face flushed red. "How'd... how'd you know about that?"

Cael laughed a bubbly laughter and tilted his head back. "Are you kidding? You're branded as the worst failure of the century! Everyone knows about it! And let me guess, you're here to try and remedy that? Get inside the dream of someone you ruined? The feeling of guilt getting to ya?" He cackled again, this time, bubbles of clouds floated out from his mouth.

"No." Heaven didn't have the energy or patience to deal with Cael's nonsense. In any other circumstance, he would've immediately stormed out of that cave, sliding back down the mountain and never looking back. But he needed him. He needed Cael to help him communicate with Lily. He had to speak to her again before it was too late, and time was running out. "It's a girl."

"Ooo, what's this? Our little Heaven is... in love? Who's the lucky gal? An angel? A fae?" He flew in closer. "Don't tell me it's a unicorn."

"A human," Heaven told him, watching as Cael's eyes widened, and his smile disappeared.

"A human? Don't you know how dangerous it is to fall in love with a human? What does God always say? NEVER fall in love with one of his creations. It compromises our mission. Especially not with a creature whose world is about to burn down! Have you gone crazy? God will have your head for sure, for sure!" The cherub was yelling almost excitedly, as if he loved the idea of Heaven getting into trouble.

"Look! I know, I know, okay? But I don't care. I need to see her... speak to her. I need her to know who I am so I can protect her before it's too late. Are you going to help me or not?"

Cael thought about it, and then nodded. "Fine, I'll help, but only because I want to see how this disaster turns out. And if God comes after me, it's your head. Got it?"

"Deal."

Honestly, he'd agree to anything at that moment. Lily was the most important thing on his mind. He had to let her know that he was there for her. That he was watching over her even while she was immersed in the apocalypse.

"Follow me."

Heaven followed suit as Cael led him into a pink room, a single chair sitting in the middle, surrounded by pink curtains and equally pink clouds.

"Wow, you really have a thing for pink."

"Shut up," Cael responded. "It's my job, not my lifestyle. Now, sit in that chair, and close your eyes. Count down slowly from ten, and imagine yourself standing at the Golden Gates."

Reluctantly, Heaven walked over to the chair and sat down, closing his eyes like Cael instructed. He took a deep breath and started counting, picturing himself standing by the bars of the gates.

Come on, Lily.

And all of sudden, there she was, standing on top of the white clouds on the other side.

"Lily! Lily!" he called out to her.

It took her a moment to register where she was, looking below her and jerking slightly backwards at the initial shock. Heaven wasn't sure how Cael made it happen, but Lily was definitely as confused as he was.

"Lily! Over here!" he called out again.

When she finally found where the voice was coming from, she walked over to the Golden Gates.

"I know you," she said. "I've seen you before."

She looked confused but utterly beautiful, and Heaven couldn't help the blush creeping up his cheeks.

Recognition lit up Lily's eyes, "Hayden?"

"My name is Heaven," he said softly. He didn't know how much time he had, so he cut straight to the facts. "I am your guardian angel, and I'm here to protect you."

"Protect me? Protect me from who?"

Heaven suddenly sprung up from the chair, opening his eyes and coming back to the awful pink room. "What happened?"

"Ohhh, I forgot to tell you," Cael answered nonchalantly. "You only have about sixty seconds inside a dream. After that, you come back to reality."

"I need to go back! I need to see her again!"

That hadn't been enough, he needed more time, he needed to return and warn Lily. Heaven's world seemed to stop for a moment, but then the cherub gave him an offer.

"Tell you what... You bring me some of those tasty bottles you're always drinking from, and I'll let you go back in."

CHAPTER
SEVEN

~ Heaven ~

Heaven did as Cael asked. The following night, he tossed a bottle over to Cael and slumped down onto the chair, closing his eyes and letting his mind rest.

"It's good seeing you again, Lily," Heaven said through the bars.

She looked as beautiful as ever.

"How do you know my name?" she asked, walking over closer to him.

"I know everything." He smiled at her, his lips

turning into an upside-down arch.

"Are you God?"

Heaven laughed, his head tilting back when he did. "No, but I am one of his right-hand men and, specifically, I'm in charge of overseeing the human world, your world."

She raised her right brow. "I don't believe you. In charge of the human world? Who exactly are you?"

"I'm your guardian angel." As if to prove his point, his ethereal wings extended from his back.

And just like that, Lily faded away again.

"This is ridiculous!" Heaven sprung out of the chair and towered over Cael, who was blissfully chugging away at his present. "There has to be a better way, a longer way to stay in communication with her. There has to be!"

"There is," Cael replied casually, "but you may not like it."

"What is it?"

"Go to the human world." Cael paused, as if letting him soak up the words. "There, you can communicate with her all you want without the fear of waking up."

Heaven shook his head. "You know I can't. If I go against the council, I'll be excommunicated from the City of God forever, banished! I can't! Losing my place was enough; I have already been taken out of my dutiful job and made a mere overseer of words. If I go against them again, they will banish me, no doubt!"

"Suit yourself." Cael shrugged, completely unconcerned. "But it's either that, or continue having these meaningless conversations that go nowhere. How much can you really do to protect her, anyway? She's all the way down there, and soon, she'll either burn in flames or get murdered by one of her own kind. Unless you're down there with her, there's not much you can do."

Cael had a point, as much as Heaven hated admitting it. But he couldn't go against the council without facing serious consequences. There was nothing else he could do other than warn her. Her impending doom was inevitable anyway, wasn't it? Her world was burning and, pretty soon, Lily and everyone else down there would be dead.

He retreated back to his home, and once on his throne, he grabbed a bottle off the marble table. The warm liquid trickled down his throat and temporarily washed away his pain.

"What's the point? I'm stupid to even think I could do anything to help her."

Gabriel then knocked on his door, yet another platter in his hands.

"How'd it go? Did you find him?"

"Yeah, yeah, I did. But it wasn't what I was expecting. It's hopeless. Not really much I can do from way up here. I guess I'll just have to sit and wait for her to die in God's flames. See where she ends up."

"Oh, stop being such a downer! You're Heaven, one of the greatest angels to ever course the skies. You deserve better than to sit around worrying about some human you barely know. Come out and party with us!"

Heaven watched as Gabriel took another sip of his champagne. He *did* have a point. His last chance of reconnecting with Lily had been nothing more than a fleeting fate, and he didn't dare go against the rules of the council to save her physically.

"Alright, let's go," he eventually agreed.

"That's my man!"

Time in the City of God moved much quicker than it did down in the human world, and Heaven felt like he'd been fixated on Lily for so long that he could barely remember the last time he'd let loose and allowed his inhibitions to disintegrate.

Club Savior was the most exclusive lounge in the entire city, so exclusive that only the angels at the top of the chain had access to it. Crystal diamonds, beautiful dancers, and a fountain of all the champagne anyone could ever drink. A few griffins could even be seen outside, probably after escorting the angels to the club. The magnificent creatures were meant to be the best soldiers in the wars to come. But with peace being the most usual state of things, they were kept almost as the most renowned pets one could have around.

The place brought back memories to Heaven. During his young and naïve days, days where he didn't constantly worry about the human strife, he'd gone there often — going home with a different dancer every night and repeating it the following day. It was truly a time of sensational pleasure, worry free, and nothing else on his mind other than pure lust. So much had changed since then.

He sat down on a purple velvet sofa when he walked in, Gabriel heading over to the bar to grab a couple drinks for them. He remembered it well, being slumped across that very same sofa not that long ago with six dancers fawning all over him. He'd felt powerful, desired, wanted, the prettiest damsels worshiping him at his feet.

But this time, it all felt different. Even with Charmaine draped around his shoulders, tugging at him to go into the private sanctuary with her, just the two of them alone, he found it easy to push her away, which shocked them both. It shocked Gabriel, too, who looked at him like he was a fool.

"What do you mean you have to go?!" Charmaine demanded after he pushed her off him.

"I can't do this. This isn't me, not anymore."

Heaven polished off the rest of his drink and walked out the door. A few of the dancers tried to stop him, tried to entice him to stick around a little longer, but he pushed them out of the way, too. Life just didn't feel fulfilled without Lily, and he wanted nothing more than to go home and sulk in his own misery.

When he got home and slouched on his throne, he tried to resist the urge to check in on Lily. He knew it would only bring more heartache and pain, longing for her when he couldn't have her. It was painful to even think about it. But the urge was too strong, pulling him closer and closer toward the mirror, and he finally gave in and told himself that one tiny peek couldn't do much damage.

"Just one little look, just one. And then I'll stop," he grumbled under his breath as he picked up the clicker.

But when he switched on the mirror, he didn't see Lily. Instead, he saw Sydal talking to a group of men wearing black masks and spiked boots.

"Of course not," Sydal was saying. "She doesn't suspect a thing. Honestly, I didn't expected her to be so stupid! I thought I'd have to try a little harder to get her to fall for me." He let out a loud laugh, and the rest joined in.

"How much longer are we gonna have to wait? She's Lilith, *the* Lilith. We need her to open the portal."

"Just... just be patient, Skin. I'm glad we finally found the right person. After killing so many others, I was beginning to question whether we even had the right city. But we'll open it soon enough. Trust me, she's not going anywhere. And after we get what we want, we'll kill her."

Skin clapped his hands together and cackled. "Finally, alas, we'll be able to fulfill the destiny of our one true leader."

Heaven quickly turned the mirror off when the rest cheered with him.

"Lily! I have to help her!"

He quickly jumped to his feet and rushed out the door, crossing the Enchanted River to the Whimsical Caves as fast as he could.

"Nice seeing you aga—" Hopscotch started to say.

"No time, Hopscotch!"

Heaven rushed up to where Cael's cave sat and knocked on the door as quickly as he could. "Cael! Cael! Open up!"

Several knocks later, the door swung open, Cael's eyes tired and weary when he greeted Heaven.

"What's wrong with you? You angels are all the same, disturbing my peace whenever you need something, like we owe it to you!"

"Cael!" Heaven panted, out of breath. "I need your help! I need you to connect me with Lily again. She's in great danger!"

But Cael only rolled his eyes. "And? How's that my problem?"

"Cael! Please!"

"Alright, alright. Wings too tight or something? But first, I want an apology."

"An apology?"

"Correct, an apology." Cael crossed his arms over his chest and turned around. "An apology, or no dream!"

"Sorry," Heaven mumbled, his impatience rising.

"What was that? You're going to have to speak up. I'm a little hard of hearing."

"I said, I'm sorry," Heaven repeated.

"You're sorry for what?"

"Oh, come on, really? I'm sorry for disturbing your peace."

"Now, that's more like it. Very well, follow me then."

Heaven quickly rushed over to the chair when they walked into the pink room and sat down, closing his eyes and picturing the Golden Gates.

"Lily, Lily! Over here!" he quickly called out when he saw.

She stormed over to the gates and demanded, "Okay, I'm tired of this. What's going on? Why do I keep coming back here?"

So cute, even when she's angry. Heaven smiled to himself. But then he shook his head. *Not the time for this!*

"You're in danger," he replied. "That man down there with you, Sydal, he's up to no good. You need to find a way to escape, run far away from him before it's too late."

She scrunched her face and pouted. "What? That's insane! Sydal's a good man. He's protecting me from the Jaguars, and he promised to help me find my sister. Why would someone evil do that?"

"You don't understand," Heaven retorted. "I know what he's capable of. He's not trying to protect you. He's been following you, and he's been manipulating you into believing him so he can swoop in and destroy you when you least expect it."

"No! *You* don't understand! You don't know anything about him!"

"Then how do you explain running into him after seeing no one else around for so long? How do you explain the headaches and migraines you've been having when you wake up every time you black out? Why has he been putting off helping you week after week? How do you explain all that, Lily?"

He'd seen so much through the mirror, and he'd been stupid not to intercede before, not to tell her that Sydal wasn't to be trusted. He'd known… the last vision had only confirmed it, but he'd known better and hadn't done anything about it.

"Stop! Stop it!" Lily threw her hands over her ears, shaking her head furiously.

"Lily! Listen to me, please! You have to believe me. You have to protect yourself!"

"Shut up! Shut up!"

Heaven's eyes sprung open, and he found himself staring at the pink walls again.

"No!" he yelled. "This can't be happening!"

"Conversation didn't go so well?" Cael asked.

Heaven shot him a look, a glare that was strong enough to melt a thousand humans. But to Cael, it was nothing but a nasty look.

"No, Cael, it went swell! Look how happy I am!" He pointed to his face. "No! It didn't go well! She's in danger! Grave danger! And I have to help her, but I don't know how, and she won't believe me!"

"Well, there's always…"

"No! No, Cael. I can't. You and I both know the consequences of going into one of God's created worlds without reason and permission. If the council ever finds out, I'd be done for!"

"Eh, whatever, suit yourself. I couldn't care less about what happens to her and that entire world. Now, if you'll excuse me, I have to get back to my nap." Cael nudged Heaven out the door of his cave and closed it behind him.

Heaven refused to give up hope. He had to save Lily from dying at the hands of Sydal. Being a homicide victim immediately prevented God's creatures from entering through the Golden Gates. Sure, there was still a chance that dying from the apocalypse meant Lily would've been trapped as Lucifer's slave, but if she were killed, she'd have no chance at all.

So, his next stop: God.

<hr>

THE ANGELS WERE USUALLY the ones who ran the Golden City. God almost never bothered unless a world was either being created or getting destroyed. And God hated it when someone disturbed him with an issue that he didn't find important, which, to be honest, were most issues. Besides, reaching God's door was another journey in itself. His throne sat on top of the highest mountain in the entire kingdom, with visitors crossing over a bridge of guilt and shame that usually forced most to turn around and deal with their problems themselves.

But Heaven knew he couldn't. He knew God was the only one who could bypass the rules of the council and allow him to go save Lily and bring her through the Golden Gates. It was a risky suggestion, bringing a creature up to the sacred kingdom, but it was important to him, and he knew he had to at least try.

But crossing that bridge was daunting, the constant voices shaming him for even thinking this was a good idea, and for risking his life for a foolish human. Tears poured from his eyes as he dealt with the guilt, but he continued to push on regardless, trying his hardest to drown out the voices. Eventually, he arrived at the yard of God's palace, a golden building decorated with the finest jewels and crystals. And in front of it, the most majestic marble Pegasus he had ever seen.

If the bridge hadn't been enough, his last obstacle was to climb up the thousand golden steps to God's door. A task almost as exhausting as the previous one. But he had to do it. He took the steps one by one, his mind focusing on the task at hand and the reward he'd get if he succeeded.

"Who dares enter my presence?" a booming voice called out when Heaven was still fifty steps away.

"It's me, God. It's Heaven... I-I need your help."

CHAPTER

EIGHT

~ Heaven ~

The huge door to the golden palace creaked open, and Heaven stepped in. He'd been inside God's palace before, but each time he stepped inside, more and more guards were present as more of his creatures either died from an apocalypse or by natural causes, and were brought into God's realm.

"They all come here," God had said to him once. "It's where the good ones belong."

"And what about the rest?" Heaven remembered asking.

93

"Well, they belong to Lucifer now. I gave them a chance when I created them. I gave them all a chance. But what they chose to do with that chance, is not my problem. If they decide to go against me, then they will forever be Lucifer's slaves. You see, Heaven, my child, Lucifer and I made a deal long, long ago. The universe used to be one controlled and united kingdom, with Lucifer ruling one side and I, the other, and still, coexisting to create a greater universe for our creations. But things went awry. Lucifer became hungry for power, attempting to overthrow my rule so he could have complete control over the entire universe. Soon, a battle broke out, two sides of one whole at war with each other to see who could claim complete control. And because of that, with both our powers conflicting, the universe severed into good and evil.

Of course, I maintained greater control, with the ability to create worlds and creatures beyond imagination, but Lucifer would be there at every step, turning my creatures against me, and bringing them into his world to create an army that he would try to use against me to seize power. All the sinners, the evil in my worlds, they're no longer welcomed into my kingdom once Lucifer has touched them. And I constantly fear the day when he finally grows his army to become strong enough to come after me and take down all that I have built. Luckily for us, he needs the portal to cross between universes, so I have some hope left."

"The portal?" Heaven had asked.

"Yes, my child, the portal. The portal can only be created if someone from Lucifer's world, a demon of some sort, either possesses someone from the Golden City itself, or someone who has ties with the Golden City. And I know all my children well; I know that no one in my kingdom would dare betray me. So even if his army continues to grow, I know my kingdom shall remain safe."

Heaven swallowed hard as his mind reflected upon God's words and returned to the present and the task at hand.

Betray. The one promise I swore to never break. And now, here I am again, tearing that bond for a human who's destined to die.

"What is it, my child?" God asked.

His voice echoed and boomed down the hall, a slight wave of wind pushing Heaven over.

Heaven closed the gap between him and the Lord, and dropped to his knees.

"Father, your highness, may I please request permission to travel to Planet Earth?"

"Planet Earth? Ha! That world is nothing but a disgrace to my name. You've done your duty. You tried to save them, but they're all nothing but a bunch of ingrates who couldn't save themselves, even if Lucifer came knocking at their front door. They're done. Time to be wiped out completely and start a new world fresh."

"But Father, please, someone is in grave danger, and I must go save her."

God stood up from his throne and walked over to where Heaven was still kneeling. As the ruler of the universe, God was much larger than the rest of the angels, his shadow towering over Heaven and all the guards as he approached.

"Save? Save her? Son, has your halo been too tight lately? Planet Earth is destined to crumble. They are facing an apocalypse. Their world is up in flames. There is no saving them. It is too late."

"Father, I know, I know. But please, I just have to save this one human, a female. I just have to."

"And why is this... female so important? Why would we give her precedence over all the other idiot humans in that idiot world?"

"Because, Father, I'm in love with her." Heaven bowed his head in shame as soon as those words left his mouth.

He expected the worst, the angry wrath of God. It was well-known that celestial beings were forbidden to fall in love with God's creatures. Sure, it had happened before, but those beings were no longer present in the City of God. Where they went, no one really knew. In the best-case scenario, banished from the universe forever. In the worst case, they became Lucifer's pawns.

"No," God simply responded.

"Father?"

"How DARE you disobey my kingdom, disobey the creed you've been sworn into? Falling in love with a creature, a human at that? The humans were the bane of my existence, turning everything I gave them against me, destroying the very fabric I'd cut them from. And now, you're asking for permission to go and save one of them because you've fallen in love? You're lucky I don't banish you over to Lucifer right now!"

"Father, I know. I know it's a terrible request to ask. I know it's a sin against all you stand for and all you've done. But all I'm asking for is one exception. If I don't save her, she'll be killed, and Lucifer will have her for sure."

"Good." God smirked and turned his back on Heaven. "Hell is where they all belong. Honestly, I don't even know why I decided to give some of them a chance to become my royal guards. They're all the same. Sickening. Now, please, I have to get back to work."

"Father, please!"

"Leave my palace. Now!"

The booming voice of God propelled Heaven straight back out through the doors and down the thousand steps. He didn't expect his plan to work, but he'd at least expected God to hear him out, given that he was one of his prized children.

But still, he refused to give up. She was the first

being in the entire universe that he'd ever felt connected to, and he wasn't going to let it go. If God wouldn't help him save Lily, he'd have to do it himself.

Later that night, when there were less eyes around, he'd go. He'd climb over the Golden Gates and enter through the portal that connected his world to the human world. He'd grab her, save her, and bring her back through the portal himself. And if God had a problem with it, then he'd have to banish both of them.

But he couldn't do it alone. The gates were heavily guarded by all the humans who had transcended during the apocalypse, and they all had strict orders to verify that all celestial beings had permission from the high council before crossing. He needed help, and there was only one angel he could turn to.

"Gabe, I need your help!" Heaven found Gabriel back at Club Savior, eating yet another platter of shrimps and surrounded by dozens of dancers. He had drunk so much that he could barely stand straight, but Heaven was desperate.

"Heaven, my man!" Gabriel greeted him when he saw him. "How about I buy you a dance?" He looked over at one of the dancers, who quickly placed her arm around Heaven, but he pushed her off.

"I need your help, Gabe, please. Can I talk to you outside? Alone?"

Gabriel let out a laugh. "*The* Heaven needs my help? Lord, have mercy. Never would I have thought

I'd hear those words coming from you. You're Heaven, the best of the best." Then he winked. "I guess that means I'm the best, right?"

"Sure, whatever, you're the best. Are you going to help me or not?"

"Step outside with me, my man. I know the most private and secluded place around here. We'll talk there!"

But instead of taking him somewhere private, Gabriel led Heaven out to the plaza that connected the club to several other bars, the busiest area he could've chosen in the entire city.

"So, tell me, what does the great and almighty Heaven want from me, the humble Gabriel?"

Heaven looked around to make sure no one was listening in, and then pulled Gabriel in closer and whispered, "I'm going to Earth."

"Wonderful! Now you can save your little girl-friend. How'd you manage to convince the high council to grant you permission?"

"I didn't." Heaven shook his head. "But I'm going anyway. I need to save her, and I don't care what it takes to do it. That's why I need your help."

"What for?"

"I need you to distract the guards, enchant them or something. Just take their attention away long enough for me to get to the portal. I'll owe you a big one for it, brother."

"Oh, my," Gabriel whispered, bringing the rest of

his martini glass up to his mouth and pouring the rest of the liquid in. "I heard that the last angel who tried to do that got instantly pulverized."

"Please, Gabe, we're best friends. I need you to do this for me! And think about it... you'll go down in history as the angel who fooled the best guards in all the skies."

"Alright, alright, I'll do it." Gabriel smirked, proud to be complimented like that.

"Thank you. I owe you. Seriously."

"Good luck, man. Find me when you get back. I have to meet this human who's got you breaking all the rules." Gabriel joked before they parted.

"Thanks, Gabe, I will."

LATER THAT NIGHT, the plan went on as expected. Gabriel was a master at enchantments, and Heaven thought he'd do a quick spell, a wave of his hands that would drop all the guards onto the clouds. But instead, as Heaven waited behind a fluffy cloud, Gabriel showed up from out of nowhere, riding one of his griffins while off-his-head drunk.

"Look at me, I'm the prettiest angel in all the skies!" he yelled at the top of his lungs as he waved what looked like a bottle of vodka in the air.

He was wearing nothing... absolutely nothing, and Heaven wondered how uncomfortable it might be to ride like that. He didn't have much time to think about it though; his window was short. As all the guards rushed to stop Gabe while he did a somersault and almost dropped off the griffin, Heaven rushed over to the unguarded portal that led to Earth and stepped in.

He had his plan set in stone in his mind: step through, find Lily, and step back in. Simple.

Only, not so simple.

As soon as Heaven stepped through, the portal behind him disappeared. He rushed to grab hold of it, unsure of why he thought it would work, but he held onto nothing but air. There was no way back in.

Anxiety rose within him, the fear of not knowing how he was going to get back home making his heart beat wildly. But either way, he had to find Lily. If she died, then all of it would've been for nothing. And he was sure God had already found out. Gabriel had probably broken down and confessed the second Heaven had stepped through the portal.

As he started to walk, he quickly realized that he didn't know where he was going. He had been able to follow Lily just fine through his mirror — the ability to identify and choose specific locations to target certainly helped. But as he stood on the incinerated streets of San Francisco, he realized he had made a huge mistake. He was ill-prepared, not a single human was in sight, and his powers could only get him so far.

"The sewers. It leads to the East District. If we can just make it over there, unseen, there's a house there we can

hide in for the time being while we figure out our next move. It belonged to my grandmother." He remembered the words spoken by Sydal that day down at the subway.

"That's it! I just have to get to the East District!" Heaven exclaimed.

But as he looked around his surroundings, there were no signs, no directions, nothing pointing to where the East District was. He didn't even know what district he was currently standing in, and whether he was facing north or south.

Then he shrugged. "No problem at all. I'll just enchant a map. I do that with everything else. Why not a map?"

When he tried the trick, his fingers looming over the palm of his other hand, nothing appeared.

"Hmm, that's odd. Must be the jet lag from traveling through that portal." He tried again, his fingers looking over his palm. Still nothing. "Come on, come on, give me a map!" Still nothing. "Ugh! This can't be happening! First, the portal disappears, and now I have no powers?"

Heaven was beginning to regret all the decisions he had ever made: from ever running into Lily and falling in love with her to deciding to go against God and come back down to a world that was destined to be destroyed. Kicking an empty soda can, he crossed the street and sat down on the curb. He needed a miracle if he wanted to find Lily. He closed his eyes, trying to picture a scenario when things could've gone worse.

"Get up, prick!"

Heaven opened his eyes to a splash of cold water on his face. He was still sitting on the curb, but the morning had turned to night, and four men, all dressed in black with spiked boots, were standing over him.

The typical outfit of Jaguars, he thought. *They're the ones after Lily.*

"Well, well, well. Look what we have here! And here I thought we'd killed all the preppy rich boys in town already."

Heaven recognized the man pointing a gun at him, Skin, the one Sydal had been talking to about killing Lily.

"What do you want from me?" Heaven asked, biding his time.

"Where have you been hiding this whole time, huh? We searched the entire fucking city of San Francisco. What'd you do, come from out of town?" Skin asked.

"Something like that. Look, man, I don't want any trouble. I'm just looking for a friend. Now, if you'll just step aside, I'll be—"

"Looking for someone? Looking for someone?! Are you blind or stupid? Do you not see everything burning down? Do you not realize that we're in the middle of an apocalypse? There's no one left alive, you idiot!" Skin moved the gun closer to him and took off the safety.

"Sydal!" he yelled.

"What?"

"Sydal! I know Sydal!"

Skin lowered the gun and stepped closer to him, sniffing around. "How do you know Sydal?"

Heaven knew he had to be quick on his feet. If he could get Skin to take him to Sydal, maybe there was a chance he'd be able to save Lily.

"Um... high school. Yeah, high school! We were classmates, friends, actually. Why do you think I'm still alive?"

Skin sniffed around again. "I smell something fishy. If you two are friends, how come he never mentioned you? I would've heard about some preppy friend..." He raised the gun again.

"No, wait! It's true. I know Sydal. He never mentioned me because we had a falling out after high school. I stole his girl... And you know how jealous he gets."

Skin chuckled. "He *does* get easily jealous."

Heaven chuckled back. "So, where is the guy? I've been looking for him, you know, I still have to make amends for the past." Then he paused and faked a tear. "Oh, no, don't tell me he died!"

Skin shook his head. "Nah, Sydal? He's still alive. In fact, he's got the ticket to Hell. But I'm sure you know all about that, given how you're his friend. Come, I'll take you to him."

As Heaven followed Skin, he couldn't help but wonder about what Skin had said. *Ticket to Hell? What did that even mean?*

Several hours later, they finally arrived at the same gas station that Sydal had taken Lily to earlier.

"What are we doing here? Is Sydal here? Seems like an odd place for him to be." Heaven took a look around.

The place was completely abandoned except for the rusty broken-down vehicle that was parked outside. And it definitely wasn't the little room with two cots that Heaven had seen Lily in.

"Just wait here," Skin said. "We gotta go get something. We'll be right back."

Heaven waited until the men were inside before he attempted to conjure his wings. All the walking had been a burden on his feet, and he needed to lift himself up to relieve his legs from the pain. With his eyes closed, he snapped his fingers. Nothing happened. He closed his eyes again, envisioning them harder this time... but still nothing. He didn't understand what was happening to him. He couldn't enchant a map, and now, he couldn't even conjure the sacred wings he'd been so blessed with. It was like... like... he'd become one of the humans.

"Hey, you! What's your name again?" Skin stuck his head out the door and called over.

"Hea-Hayden."

"Hayden, cool name. Listen, can you come in here, please? I need your help with something."

Heaven was so close. He could almost sense Sydal's presence. And he hadn't given up everything, his home, his wings, his powers, to walk away with nothing. Finding Lily was his last chance to redeem himself. He was willing to do anything he could.

And so, he did. He walked in through the glass door into the convenience store. It was completely empty, not a morsel of food or drink in sight. Even the bare shelves had all fallen down, forming mini piles of wreckage on the tiled floor. He couldn't even begin to guess why Skin had called him in here. There was nothing here!

"Hey, man, what did you need help with?"

But when Heaven turned around, he wasn't met with the face he was expecting. Instead, he was met with one of the metal shelves, colliding straight into his face.

Heaven toppled over from the impact and fell onto his back. A sharp pain shot up his spine and straight into his neck. He had seen humans get hurt before, such a comical experience to watch, but he never thought he'd have to experience it for himself.

"Sydal would never associate with a prep," Skin said, standing over him and pointing a gun at his head. Then he looked up. "Bag him."

Heaven watched in horror as three men leaned

over and threw a black plastic bag over his head, tied him up while kicking him around, and soon, he found his body being lifted off the ground and thrown into the trunk of a car. The loud thud of metal scraped against his ears, and he could barely stay upright as the movement of the vehicle threw his body from left to right.

When the car finally stopped moving, he was still shaking from the sudden surprise. He shouldn't have let his guard down. He should never have trusted Skin or any other member of the Jaguars. He was a fool to think someone like them would ever help him. And it wasn't like he could fight back, defend himself. He had no powers, and he certainly couldn't escape — he was useless without his angelic magic. Even if he got out, there was nowhere for him to go.

They didn't remove the bag until they were well inside a building. The wind had stopped blowing, and the sound had been replaced by an echo of steps. Heaven didn't know where he was, but he had a strong feeling that he was about to meet his death. But then again, maybe death wouldn't be such a bad idea. He had, after all, failed in all his missions. What else was there to really live for?

"What are we gonna do with him, boss?" He heard one of the men ask. It sounded raspy, like Skin, but he wasn't sure.

"Just leave him. He's weak. Not like he's going to do any harm. We'll deal with him later."

Sydal. Heaven was sure that was Sydal's voice. It had to be. He'd listen to it so many times; there was no way he could ever forget the voice that made his blood boil.

"Ha! Yeah, you're right, boss. I bet he can't even fight off a kid."

Heaven grunted his teeth. He was a child of God, and had sworn to forever protect and never harm, but if he had his powers right now, they'd both be flying out of the building and straight to Hell.

The two men continued laughing and laughing, until their voices grew lower, followed by the slam of a door behind them. Heaven listened for a little longer before confirming that he was indeed alone. He bowed his head down and shook the bag off from his head. He couldn't even begin to imagine the mess his hair was in as he gasped for air. Heaven had been so used to living a life of luxury and granted wishes at his command that this experience was beginning to humble him. His selfishness to save Lily for himself had put him into this; so, he had to figure out a way to get out.

"Wait," he whispered, looking around. "I know this place." He closed his eyes and tried harder to picture it. "Lily! She's in here. I have to find her! But how?"

His wrists and ankles were both tied together, and he knew he didn't have the supernatural strength he would normally have to break himself free. Looking around once more, he found a sharp nail sticking out from a rusty fireplace that looked like it hadn't been used in nearly a century, and hopped over.

"This has to work. It just has to!"

Carefully, he bent down and backed himself up against the nail, moving his body up and down in an attempt to tear the rope in half. It was painfully strenuous, his legs growing weaker and weaker, but he refused to give up.

"Come on, come on!" He moved his body faster and faster, bullets of sweat pouring from his head, and blood dripping from where the rope had strained against his skin. "Come on, break! Break!"

He continued to move, and fortunately, his final pull to the finish snapped the rope in half, and his body tumbled onto the ground.

Lucky for him, he'd seen enough of the place to know his way around, constantly following Sydal through the two-story home through the mirror that he knew exactly where Lily was being held. His only problem, getting to her without being seen.

Quickly, he untied the rope around his ankles and quietly creaked open the door. Skin and Sydal, or any of the other Jaguars, were nowhere to be seen. Heaven carefully tiptoed down the hall until he found the stairs that led down into the door he needed, and turned the knob.

And there she was. As beautiful as the day he first saw her. Even in strife, she was still a pearl in his eyes.

"Hello, Lily," he said when he walked in.

Her head sprung up at the sound of his voice, and she looked around before landing her eyes on him, blinking several times.

"Hayden?" she asked.

CHAPTER

NINE

~ Lily ~

"Hi, Lily. No, it's me, Heaven," the man replied. But Lily knew better than to be fooled so easily. She could never forget a man who'd crushed her heart into smithereens. There was no doubt in her mind that the man standing before her was Hayden Maxwell, and she wanted nothing to do with him, especially after he'd made her fall in love with him so fully, only to leave her behind without a single word. Without a goodbye. Banished into thin air.

She'd rather die at the hands of Sydal than run back to him. She wouldn't fall that low.

"Bullshit, Hayden. I know it's you. Heaven's not real. Why'd you ditch me? I actually liked you, and you just ghosted me." She paused, the heaviness of the situation dawning on her. "What are you doing here? How'd you find me?"

And how come he was still alive?

"Lily, please, listen to me. It's really me, Heaven. It's been me all along. The man you thought you met that day, Hayden... He doesn't exist; it was just a made-up name... It has always been me."

"You said that was just a stupid nickname... You said your name was Hayden." It couldn't be real. The visions couldn't be real, because, what would that mean? It made no sense. "What the hell is going on?" She whimpered.

"Why are you lying to me? Haven't you hurt me enough?!"

"No, Lily, I'm not trying to hurt you, I swear! It's a little difficult to explain, but please, you have to listen to me. This isn't what you think."

"Then what is it, Hayden? Or Heaven, whatever your name is. And those dreams... was that really you? Were those real?"

"The dreams were the only way I could communicate with you... They were real, Lily. I fought my way to come here, but I had to talk to you. I'm here now, here to save you. You have to believe me, Lily. Sydal is not a good man. He will use you, and then kill you. I've heard it all myself. We need to get you out of here."

Well, she was chained to a bed and concussed, so she'd already figured that much. But how did Hayden — or Heaven, or whoever — knew any of it?

"Hear it? How'd you even know I was here? Were you spying on me?"

Before Heaven had a chance to reply, the door kicked open. Sydal stood there, out of his street clothes, and now dressed in full Jaguar attire.

"I see our little friend here is being a bit nosy," he sneered. He cocked his gun and walked toward them.

"Wait!" Heaven shouted. "Don't come any closer unless you want to get hurt!"

Lily looked back and forth between the two men in front of her, at a loss of what was going on.

CHAPTER
TEN

~ Heaven ~

Heaven knew he didn't have any powers, not outside of the Golden City, but a part of him still hoped that if he wished for it hard enough, he might be able to conjure an enchantment to get both him and Lily out. He had to do *something*.

Sydal let out a cackle and shook his head. "And what if I do? What are you gonna do about it?" He held up the gun. "You're powerless. Weak. A nobody. How do you expect to save someone if you can't even save yourself?"

Sydal didn't even know him. Why was he talking like he knew who he was?

"Stand back, I mean it. And no one will get hurt," he continued threatening him, hoping that could be enough to get them out of there.

When Sydal started walking even closer, Heaven held out his palms, waving his fingers like he'd normally do when enchanting another living being.

"Ha! Pathetic!" Sydal cackled again when nothing happened. He forcefully lunged toward Heaven, tackling him onto the ground.

Heaven tried his hardest to fight back, pushing the man off him and twisting his body free, but Sydal was much too strong. He was quickly able to put Heaven in a lock hold and call over the others to chain him up beside Lily.

"Now, you can be with your little girlfriend, like you wanted all along." Sydal laughed.

"I'm not his girlfriend," Lily interjected, still chained and bound, an angry scowl on her face.

A pinch of pain ached in Heaven's heart — he had risked everything he had for this woman, this lowly human he had foolishly fallen in love with, and now she was acting like he was a nobody, like their relationship meant nothing to her.

"Why are you doing this?" she then asked Sydal. "What do you want from me? He said you're going to kill me..." She gestured to Heaven. "Is that true?"

"See, boss." Skin jumped in. "Told you there's something fishy about this guy. How does he know so much?"

Sydal looked over at Heaven and shrugged one shoulder, but something in his eyes told Heaven he knew more than he was letting out. "Doesn't matter. He won't be able to stop me. And you're right, Lily, or should I say... Lilith. I *am* going to kill you, just like I killed your sister."

Heaven was taken aback. *Lilith, where have I heard that name before?*

"Imalia?" Lily whispered, "You killed Imalia?"

Tears were gathering in her eyes, and Heaven wished he could do something to help.

"Of course, why else do you think I kept stalling on helping you find her? I already knew where she was." He leaned in closer and whispered in her ear. "Rotting in the next room over." Sydal pulled a thin silver necklace out from his pocket. It had a crescent pendant attached to the end, and upon seeing it, Lily paled. "Look familiar?"

Lily jerked forward, trying to attack Sydal, but the chains kept her in place. "You monster!"

"You know, Lily, it's such a shame that things have to end this way... I quite enjoyed that kiss we shared. You reminded me a lot of your sister. For a short while, I thought she was the one... I kept my eyes on both of you for a long time, looking for the person I needed to help my boss… but it was soon obvious that she wasn't the one. But oh well, that didn't stop me from having some fun."

"You pig!" Lily jerked forward again, red marks showing on her wrists as she struggled against the chains. "I swear, if I ever get out of these chains, I'm destroying every single last one of you!"

"Hmm, I don't think you will. Your time is running out, my dear."

"I will end you," Heaven threatened him.

Sydal turned his head to look over at Heaven. "You think I'm stupid, don't you? You think I don't know who you are. But oh, I do, very well, Heaven." Sydal got closer, looking him up and down with renewed inter-est. "Who you are, what you are…. who your father is. I know everything."

How? How could he know?

"And I know all about your little crush on Lily here, too. I've been spending time with her in the shadows for longer than you've known her, Heaven. We didn't think it would ever be possible for one of you to really get here… the link that ties both the kingdom of God and Lucifer together, so perfectly in sync." Sydal let out a horrific laugh, looking up to the ceiling, and then down to the floor. "Knowing about it is one thing, but seeing you here is different… It all just makes sense, I guess. It's just too bad that it took an apocalypse for us to finally put our plan into action."

It was now Lily's turn to look at Heaven. "Hayden, what's he talking about?"

"You mean, *you* don't even know?" Sydal asked Lily, a smirk plastered on his face. "I thought he would have told you the truth. But it turns out you don't even know who he *really* is? Wow, this is just too perfect! You see, my dear Lily, Heaven here, is an angel... A fantasy creature and child of God who we all thought, as kids, were just myths, but you'd be surprised to know how much of what we've been told over the years are actually real. Right, Heaven?"

"Hayden? I mean, Heaven, is this true?"

Tears welled in Lily's eyes as she looked at Heaven. He wanted so badly to rush over to her and hold her, to tell her everything was going to be okay. But even he couldn't make that promise.

"How did you find out?" he asked Sydal. *How does this man know so much about me?*

"Almost by accident, actually. For higher beings, you really need to work on blending in more. Ten days before our world blew up in flames which, I believe, was a doing of your God, I saw you. I've known about your kind for a while, but I still had my doubts; faith is a complicated thing. But the way you quickly soared over to Lily at a remarkable and impossible speed just to keep her from falling flat on her face was impressive. I knew there was something otherworldly about you, I had my suspicions... And when you decided to come back, when my men told me where and how they found you, like you'd just shown up out of thin air, I knew. Also, the only way you could've escaped from my men was in another world," he added proudly.

"Why didn't you tell us, boss?" Skin interjected, almost sounding upset.

"Shut up, Skin. I serve a higher purpose. I don't need to tell you everything I know," he snapped, making the man take several steps back. It was clear that Sydal was the one in command of the Jaguars, not even letting his team know everything he knew.

But who was Sydal serving?

There was no point denying any of it, or trying to convince them otherwise. There was only one thing that mattered, and that was getting Lily out, even if she acted like she didn't care about him. So, Heaven said the only thing he could think of.

"You can have me, Sydal, but let her go."

"Oh, I don't think so. Love is such a precious thing... It's such a shame that your little relationship was nothing more than the demise of your father's kingdom. You see, Lilith here holds my portal to your world, and I need that portal to help my boss fulfill his dream." He turned to Lily and winked. "Remember Maria, the woman you bumped into?" he asked softly. "Lilith! If you can hear me, the time is now!" he yelled in a deep voice, staring right into Lily's eyes.

Heaven gasped. *Lilith? No, this can't be right.*

Lilith was Lucifer's well-known consort, and a very dangerous woman as well as soul-taker. She had been known throughout history to take human bodies for her ill-doings, a hard look into their eyes, allowing her space into their mind.

But that couldn't be true. Lily, *his* Lily… she couldn't have run into Lilith, could she?

Your time is done, my child. It is now my turn to rule. The thought pressed itself into Heaven's mind, like a voice coming out from Lily, but her lips never moved.

Lily let out a loud shriek, and a ray of light shot straight out from her mouth, followed by a cloud of darkness. Her eyes were turned back, showing only white, and her hands were trembling by her sides.

A portal.

But instead of a portal that would lead them back into the Golden City, the light opened a different portal, one of fire and fury, one that led an army of undead straight into the portal at God's kingdom. A triple frontier, joining all of their worlds. It was a terrifying view, one that churned Heaven's stomach.

Sydal was laughing again. "Finally! Lucifer has risen! The kingdom of God shall perish forever, and the entire universe will bow down to Lucifer as their sole leader!"

"No," Heaven whispered as a wave of demons soared through the Gates of Hell and into the Golden

City, striking down all the guards and burning through the kingdom like a raging phoenix.

He rushed over to try and close the portal, but even with Lily's mouth shut, the demons continued to soar into God's universe, taking down angel after angel as Lucifer's army grew. Lily's body went limp, and Heaven could barely feel the thumping of her heart. At least, she was still alive.

"It's too late now," Sydal sneered as he smirked at him. "There's no saving either of them. Lilith no longer needs a vessel to keep the portal open; once it's triggered, the link between the two universes will remain open until Lucifer's army wins! And now, Lilith is free, as well as Lucifer! Your world is ours!"

Feeling powerless, Heaven grabbed Lily's limp body and leapt through the portal to the Golden City. Maybe there was a chance he'd get his powers back and could join the other celestial beings in this war — it was the only hope he had. He was sure God already knew what was happening, and he'd probably banish Heaven forever once he discovered that it was his all fault, but still, he had a kingdom to fight for, and he refused to just cower and run away.

Once he arrived through the gates, luckily, his wings returned, and so did his powers as he conjured an enchantment that made eight demons collapse instantly. He had much more that he needed to do, but first, he had to get Lily to safety. If he could get her back to his palace, he wouldn't need to worry about her and could focus solely on defeating Lucifer's army.

But as he soared through the sky, he failed to see Lilith come up from behind him. She struck him down, and Lily fell out of his arms.

"Lily!"

He tried to go after her, flying down as fast as he could, but Lilith was too fast and too strong for him, charging straight at him and tackling him to the ground.

When he came to, it was uncanny to see that Lilith, Lucifer's lover, had a striking similarity to Lily. Her chestnut-brown hair draped smoothly down her back and over her shoulders, and the way she walked was with grace. But her eyes were red, and evil, and Heaven knew he had to forget all the memories he had with Lily if he stood any chance of taking this demon down.

"Why so brash, my dear Heaven?" she asked, gracefully floating over to him while he stood in a fighting position. "I thought we had such a great time together. The laughter. Sharing secrets. The kiss." She winked at him.

"I will never kiss you," Heaven grumbled sternly.

"Oh, but you have. And I bet you'd like to do it again." She aggressively grabbed Heaven by the neck and kissed him hard on the lips, her snake-like tongue forcing its way in between his lips and wrapping around his own tongue.

He closed his eyes, her lips so similar to Lily's that he felt his body giving in.

"That's it," Lilith whispered. "Submit to me." She massaged his lips against hers, sliding her hands up and down his body, until she suddenly choked and spat out blood. As she slowly turned her head, she found a dagger stuck straight through her neck, green smoke coming from it. "Is that...?"

"Poison?" Heaven finished for her. "Yes, yes it is."

He smiled as Lilith's body sunk to the ground, and her face turned to stone before crumbling. "You really think you could ever replace the love of my life? You disgusting hag!"

He threw the dagger down on top of her and went looking for Lily.

"Lily! Lily! Where are you?" he called out.

The war continued to rage on behind him, Gabriel clumsily leading his army of griffins while Michael led his army of phoenixes. Heaven watched with guilt as many of the celestial beings fell to their deaths, Lucifer's army too powerful to be taken down. Gabriel was clearly still under the influence of alcohol, his movements jerky and uncoordinated. He landed close by, and Heaven made his way to him as fast as he could.

They weren't prepared for this kind of battle, and Heaven wasn't sure how to help. There was nothing they could do to win except...

The Sword of a Thousand Warriors.

"Gabriel, quick, what's the status?"

"We're losing... badly. I don't... I." Gabriel ran a hand down his face. "I can't think clearly; I don't know what else to do to turn the tides."

"What about the sword?" Heaven asked, "Why haven't you gone to get it yet?"

Gabriel's usual smug expression fell, and he was left looking like the insecure little boy Heaven had known him to be a long time ago.

The Sword of a Thousand Warriors possessed the strength of the greatest warriors since the beginning of time, the ones who fought to keep the universe from falling into the hands of evil, and the ones who sacrificed their lives to keep the universe safe. The sword had never been touched by any of the celestial beings before, kept safe for this very moment, the battle against Lucifer that had been predicted since the beginning of time. As God's most trusted, only Gabriel and Heaven knew of its whereabouts and how to get it. God had told them that only his most loyal could obtain the sword.

"I tried...," Gabriel said in such a small voice that Heaven barely heard him.

"What happened?!"

"I-I couldn't get it."

Heaven's mind went blank. If Gabriel couldn't get the sword, then they were doomed. Doomed to all perish under Lucifer's army. He slumped, the weight of the world on his back suddenly feeling too much.

But then Gabriel put a hand on his shoulder and squeezed hard. "I couldn't get to the top, brother, but I think you should go. You should try."

"What are you talking about?"

"You should go and get the sword, save us all."

"I can't do that!" Heaven replied desperately. "I have been dethroned, removed from my rightful place by God's side. There's no way I can get the sword if you can't!"

"Look at me!" Gabriel slapped a hand against his own chest. "I've been drinking like a fool while you've been trying to find a way to still save what all of us thought was hopeless... The Sword of a Thousand Warriors feeds on the hope of its people... I believe in you, brother. Now, believe in yourself."

A minute passed, in which the battle around them raged on, angels and demons alike falling to their demise all over the place. And then, like a slap to the face, Heaven snapped out of his stupor.

"Look out for Lily if you see her," he said as a way of goodbye.

And then he pushed past Gabriel and ran toward the Forbidden Tower, where they safeguarded the sword.

"If we all make it out of this alive, I won't even care if Father never speaks to me again. It's all my fault."

The stairs inside the tower seemed infinite, step after step in a too narrow tower where Heaven couldn't extend his wings. The tower had been built like that on purpose, to stop undeserving angels from flying to the top. He felt like time was slowing down as his legs grew heavy with exhaustion, but he kept pushing. He had to save Lily, and in order to do that, he had to save God's kingdom.

His hands were on the steps, helping him push up, when he suddenly reached up and fell on his face. Heaven looked up from his bleeding hands and scabbed knees to find a small round room with glistening and polished floors. And right there, in the middle, the Sword of a Thousand Warriors. It was a sight to behold, but Heaven didn't have much time. He rushed to the center of the room as fast as his legs would carry him and grabbed the base of the sword. With a too-simple but too-heavy pull, he lifted the sword over his head and rested it over his shoulder as he moved toward the large window that overlooked the entire kingdom.

For how long he thought it had taken him to get up, the tower didn't seem that high. He could see the battle raging below, Gabriel still leading his army of griffins while Michael soared with his phoenixes on the other side. Each of them holding a front. Each of them struggling to keep the demons at bay.

Without thinking about it too much, Heaven aimed the sword toward the army of the undead. "This better work."

With one swift motion and all his strength, he threw the sword straight into the middle of the battlefield, the blade sticking into the ground and sending out a beam of light so strong that Heaven had to shield his eyes for a moment. When the light dimmed, he could see that the celestial light had incinerated Lucifer's army, and it was now slowly closing the portal, it's edges closing bit by bit, as if the light was sewing it shut.

Heaven fell to his knees.

He couldn't believe it had worked. He'd always thought it was a myth, something God made up so his children would feel more secure if Lucifer were to ever invade their land — a children's tale. But it had really worked, and he had managed to wield the sword.

He didn't have time to think about what it meant. After taking only a moment to catch his breath, he got up and flew over to the center of the battlefield. He had to find her.

The place was a complete bloodbath. Bodies from both sides laid scattered across the land... including Lily's.

Heaven's face fell, and he rushed over to her side, picking up her head and holding it in his hands. "Lily, please, no." While creatures who died in their own worlds had the chance of entering either universe, those who died in the City of God were gone forever. He lowered his forehead and leaned it against hers. "I'm so sorry, Lily. I did everything I could to try and save you. I've failed."

"Heaven." A booming voice was heard behind him.

Heaven turned around, and God was standing beside him, along with Gabriel, Michael, and the remaining angels, all carrying the fallen victims of the war.

He bowed his head. "I'm sorry, Father. I have failed you."

"You have, but you also managed to take down Lucifer's army. Now, we no longer have to live in fear."

"But at what cost?" Heaven looked back down at Lily, running his fingers through her hair. "I've lost the one thing I tried so hard to protect. Father, please, can you save her?"

God shook his head. "I'm sorry, son. It is impossible to revive the dead, especially if they die in the celestial kingdom. If I could, I wouldn't be burying all my fallen men."

"Alright, Father, I understand."

Tears began to fall from Heaven's eyes, an emotion that he didn't even think he was capable of expressing.

"But that doesn't mean there isn't a way to save her... a sacrifice," God continued.

"Sacrifice?"

"Your enchanting powers... Channel them all into the human, and the force generated will be enough to save her. But be warned, it also means—"

"That I'll no longer be an angel."

Heaven knew exactly what God meant, something he never thought he'd have to resort to. He loved being a celestial being, having that much power over the universe, and the freedom to do as he desired. It was all he'd ever known, and he never thought anything else would become more important. But that all changed.

"I'll do it," he said confidently. "Whatever it takes to save her."

"Very well," God replied. "Thy wish be done."

CHAPTER
ELEVEN

"Hayden, I need three copies of this report on my desk by noon."

"Yes... yes, sir. I mean, Mr. Barbosa. I'm on it."

Hayden Maxwell stood up from his desk and rushed over to the copy room. His wedding anniversary was tonight, and he had to rush through work if he wanted to make it home in time. He didn't want his wife getting mad at him. It was physically painful whenever he had to deal with her wrath, like she became some sort of supernatural creature when she didn't get her way.

As far as Hayden could remember, he'd lived in Starwood his entire life, meeting his wife, Lily, in high school, getting married soon after, and buying a house together. And because of that, he had to take the first job he could find, as a stockbroker. It wasn't the luxurious lifestyle he had dreamt of, being a pilot, soaring high in the sky and feeling like he was living in the clouds, but it paid well, and it was enough to keep Lily satisfied. It's all he ever wanted. After all, it truly was about a happy wife, happy life.

"Hayden Maxwell, your wife, Lily Maxwell, is on the other line," a voice announced from his blazer pocket.

He pulled out the glowing orb from his pocket and pressed against the top. A holographic projection of Lily appeared.

"Hey, honey, don't forget to pick up a bottle of champagne on your way home tonight. I have a very special dinner waiting for you," she said.

"Got my reminder right here!" Hayden patted the breast pocket of his blazer. "I'll be home by six. Not a second later."

"I'll be waiting." And then the projection disappeared.

Hayden glanced over at the clock. He only had an hour left, and it takes exactly thirty-eight minutes to get home. Quickly, he pulled the papers from the copier, stapled each set together, and hurried into Mr. Barbosa's office.

"Here are your copies, sir." He placed the papers on his desk and stepped back. "And if it's alright with you, I'd like to clock out now. The wife is waiting at home with our anniversary dinner. You know how wives can get."

His boss smiled at him. "Oh, I know that very well, all too well. If I had hurried home to my wife instead of stopping for a drink, maybe she wouldn't have left me." His smile then turned into a frown as he reflected on his past. "What are you still standing here for? Go!"

"Yes, sir. See you tomorrow."

Hayden rushed over to his desk and picked up his briefcase. He then scanned his ID on his way out, changing from his office clothes into his normal streetwear of a white leather jumpsuit with tall boots and a fedora. It wasn't really by choice. All the men in Starwood wore the same thing, but it never bothered Hayden either way. It was just something to cover his body. No point in being selective about it.

"Oops, my apologies," he said, scooting out of the way for a man who was walking toward him.

He made his way down the steps and into a pod.

"Liquor store, please," he spoke into the receiver and entered his password.

Everyone in Starwood had their own unique code that either granted or denied them access to different areas throughout the city. Those of the upper class had access to their own personal drivers, the ability to ride the pods that soared across the sky and bypassed traffic, while those of the lower class, like Hayden, had to settle for public pods that had a tendency to occasionally break down. But private transportation was a luxury in Starwood, and only the most exclusive had access to them.

Even so, Hayden never complained too much. He lived in the heart of the city, and everything he needed, including the office, was within a short distance from his home. Just another average citizen, he was, and he wouldn't have it any other way.

When the pod finally came to a stop, he inserted a chip into the slot and stepped off.

"I really need to start curbing my spending," he mumbled, looking down at the chips in his hand.

Only four left. Chips acted as the currency for citizens of Starwood. Households were only allotted ten a month, and Hayden had already spent more than half, with still three weeks left to go.

He shrugged, shoved the chips back into his pocket, and walked inside the liquor store. He had to focus on getting home to his wife.

"Hello!" The shopkeeper greeted when Hayden walked in. "How may I help you?"

Hayden pulled out his chips and counted them again, secretly hoping more would appear. He sighed. "What can I get for two chips? Champagne."

"Two? Two chips? That's not very much. Let me

check in the back. Maybe there's something old in the inventory that we can part with. I'll be right back."

Hayden nodded and looked around the store as the shopkeeper disappeared. There were signs everywhere, just like in his home, in his office, and all over town, signs reminding citizens to know their place and obey the law. Hayden had never seen it in his lifetime, but rumor had it that anyone who dared step out of bounds, well, they were never seen or heard from again. Such a chilling thought to even think about. He could never rebel against the law like that.

Five minutes later, the shopkeeper returned from the back. "Well, I couldn't find much, but I did find this small bottle of champagne. It's only good for one serving, so I hope you'll be having this alone."

"Not me," Hayden replied. "My wife, but I guess this will have to do." He fished two chips out from his pocket and placed them in the shopkeeper's hand. "Hopefully, she's already had some and won't notice."

"Good luck, son. Thy wish be done."

Hayden mumbled his thanks and gave the old man a confused look before walking out. It wasn't his place to question the words of others, but he could've sworn he'd heard that phrase before. And not from the shopkeeper. This was his first time ever stepping foot in the place.

He hopped back into a pod and headed home.

"Only one chip left," he sighed when he got out and walked inside his house.

Bodega Heights was the most popular and crowded condominium in all of Starwood. It was where most of the working class stayed, as it remained in close proximity to the grocery store, the bank, and even the mall. But still, Hayden continued to dream of the day when he could move into Northern Cross, the elite community reserved for the best. But his dream always remained a dream. He was born into this class. It didn't matter how hard he tried to change it; it just wasn't going to happen.

Tucking the bottle of champagne in his elbow, Hayden headed into the common space to check his mailbox. He didn't receive mail often, usually just bills and notices reminding him to obey the law. His neighbors were often there, sipping on cans of beer and talking about their days, and Hayden sometimes liked to join in on their conversation.

"Hey, Hayden," one of them called out to him as he grabbed the stack of papers from his mailbox.

"Mark," Hayden nodded in reply. "Haven't seen you down here in a while."

Mark shrugged. "Yeah, blame it on the wife. She's got me spending all my chips with her crazy errand requests. I haven't been able to go anywhere in two weeks because I have nothing left. But what can you do about it, right? Women, they own us."

"I guess." Hayden tried to hide the bottle of champagne behind his back, hoping Mark wouldn't notice it.

"I see you got another bottle there. Oh, boy, Lily is going to be angry for sure when she finds out that she's not getting the big one."

Crap, he noticed.

"I know, I know. But this was all I could afford. Maybe one day, when I finally get that promotion, I'll have enough to buy her the things she wants."

"Dream big, Hayden. Dream big. But men like us, the most we can ask for is to not end up in the Hive. I hear the citizens there don't get any chips! Imagine that. Trying to survive in this world without any chips. I'd rather die."

"Hayden Maxwell, your wife, Lily Maxwell, is on the other line," a voice announced from his blazer pocket.

"I have to run. Otherwise, Lily is going to blow a fuse. But it was nice seeing you again. Talk soon?" Hayden jumped up from the lounge chair and ran quickly over to the exit.

"Good luck, man," Mark shouted back.

As Hayden quickly hurried up the stairs, he tripped on a step and toppled over, the papers in his hand flying onto the ground.

"No, no, no. This can't be happening." He rushed over to pick up the newspapers and brochures, but an unmarked envelope caught his eye.

He picked it up, surprised by the lightness for its size. And when he flipped it over, it was sealed with a stamp that said, "Heaven."

"What is this?" he whispered to himself.

"Hayden Maxwell, your wife, Lily Maxwell, is on the other line," a voice announced from his blazer pocket.

"Ugh!" He scooped up the rest, tucked them under his arm, and ran down the hall.

"Hey, honey, Lily. I'm so sorry I'm late. I tripped on the stairs on the way up, and papers went flying everywhere." He placed the mini bottle of champagne and the stack of papers on the kitchen counter. "Lily?" he called out again when no one answered. "Lily? Where are you?"

Hayden searched through all the rooms until he finally found his wife huddling in the corner beside the toilet. She was rocking her body back and forth, her eyes bloodshot from the tears she had cried.

"Honey? Honey, what's wrong?" He rushed over next to her and pulled her into an embrace.

"I... I had a nightmare. But it felt so real! Like something, a monster or something, went inside of me and started telling me to do all these bad things." Lily broke down and started sobbing uncontrollably, her body shaking from the fear.

He wrapped his arms even tighter around her. "It's okay, it's okay. It was just a bad dream. You're okay now." He kissed her gently on the cheek. "Now, come on, we have an anniversary to celebrate."

LATER THAT NIGHT, after Lily had gone to bed and Hayden began clearing up the dirty dishes, he glanced over at the stack of mail he had collected earlier.

The envelope.

He dried his hands and went over to pick it up. He had never received anything so mysterious before. And the stamp on the back... He'd never seen anything like it. Dare he open it? What if it was meant for someone else? What if it was someone playing a prank on him? What if it was an urgent letter from the government issuing his arrest? Taking a deep breath, he slowly peeled it open. Inside, was a single sheet of paper written in gold ink.

"Hayden!" Lily suddenly shouted from the bedroom.

He dropped the paper back down on the kitchen table and rushed over to her, grabbing a bat from the hall as he ran.

"Who's here? What is it? I'll knock his brains out!"

"I saw her again!" she yelled in tears.

"Saw who?"

"The monster! She had red eyes, and fangs, and she said she's going to kill me!"

Hayden dropped the bat and cuddled beside his wife in bed. "You just had another bad dream, sweetie. Monsters aren't real. You know that. Besides, I'm right here next to you. I promise I won't let anything happen to you."

Lily looked up at him, her eyes wide and innocent. "Do you swear?"

"I swear." He leaned down and kissed her on the forehead. "I swear it with my life."

Hours later, he was awoken by a loud shriek. He sprung out of bed and found Lily standing in front of the bathroom mirror, clawing at her eyes. It looked as if she had seen a ghost, haunted by whatever nightmare she was having. Her face was completely pale, and her body felt cold when he touched her.

"Lily! Stop!" Hayden ripped her hands away from her face.

"Get her out of me! Get her out of me!" Lily collapsed onto the floor, pulling Hayden down with her. She buried her head into his chest and clawed at his arms before he finally pulled her away.

"That's it," he said sternly. "We're going to see Dr. Feldman first thing in the morning."

THE SINGLE SHEET of paper with gold writing had moved when Hayden woke up the next morning... to his bedside table. He managed to make out the words "please read" before rushing out the door with Lily wrapped in a blanket, still shivering from the events of the previous night. Lucky for them, she still had some chips, saving them the long walk to Dr. Feldman's office.

Dr. Christopher Feldman was the best, and the only, psychiatrist in Starwood. He didn't see many patients, only the few rare nutcases who steered away from the standard norm. He was old, his hair graying, and glasses so low that Hayden wondered how he managed to even see through them. His office was calming when they walked in, the trickling fountain soothing his nerves, and the warm air bringing Lily back down to her senses.

"Everything's going to be okay," Hayden reassured his wife before leading her over to the lounge chair.

But as they walked by a mirror, Lily jumped and gasped. "She's here!"

She nearly collapsed onto the ground, but Hayden caught her just in time. "Who's here?"

"The... the monster! I saw her!" She pointed over to the mirror, but when Hayden walked over, he could only see his own reflection.

They both jumped at the sound of a knock on the door, relieved when they saw Dr. Feldman walk in instead of whatever monster Lily had been expecting.

"Ah, Mr. and Mrs. Maxwell. How are you two doing on this beautiful sunny day?" Dr. Feldman was dressed in the same white leather jumpsuit and fedora as Hayden was. The only difference was the white overcoat that draped over his shoulders.

"Um, good, doctor. My wife here has been having nightmares lately, recurring nightmares about some sort of monster. I think it might be stress or something, maybe anxiety." Hayden gestured over to Lily, who was rocking back and forth in the chair, jerking her body like she was trying to avoid something.

"Hmm, interesting. I usually hear stories where someone is falling off a building or drowning, never anything about monsters." He reached his pen up to scratch his nose. Then he turned his head over to face Lily. "Tell me, Lily, what does this monster look like? Can you describe it for me?"

Still shaking, Lily tried to speak. "She... she has sharp teeth, uh... red eyes, black skin. She looks like... like... THAT!" Lily gasped and pointed in a direction behind the doctor.

Hayden shot his head up, but only saw the white wall. So did Dr. Feldman, as he tried to calm down the hallucinating Lily and told her that nothing was there.

The rest of the session proved to be unproductive, so Dr. Feldman gave Hayden a bottle of suppressants to take home with them and sent them on their way. Hayden couldn't figure out what was wrong with his wife as they climbed into a pod to go home. She was usually so level-headed, the rational one out of the two, but for some reason, she had gone crazy.

When they arrived home, he carried her straight to bed, gave her a pill, and retreated to the kitchen to make her some soup. Maybe a warm meal would be enough to bring down her anxiety. As he set the bowl of chicken noodle soup down on the bedside table, he noticed the sheet of paper.

"Please read," it said again at the top.

Hayden pulled out the sheet, folded it, and shoved it into his pocket before sitting beside his wife and scooping a spoonful of the soup into her mouth.

"Eat this, honey," he said. "It'll make you feel better."

"Am I crazy?" Lily asked him, her eyes watery and red.

He shook his head. "No, of course not. You just need to get some rest. I'm sure you'll feel better in the morning."

When the bowl was empty, he tucked his wife into bed and brought the dirty dish back into the kitchen. He fixed himself a cold turkey sandwich and sat down at the kitchen table to enjoy his lunch alone. Even since he got married, not a single day had gone by where he felt alone in his home. Lily was always there by his side, sharing stories and jokes with each other.

After he took his first bite, Hayden pulled the sheet of paper from his pocket and unfolded it.

"Please read," he said, reading the words out loud. "Your name is not Hayden Maxwell. You are not who you think you are." He continued to read. "Your real name is Heaven, and Lucifer has put a spell on you. The world you are living in isn't real. Wake up! Wake up, and save yourself."

Suddenly, he heard a scream from their bedroom. Hayden dropped the note and rushed in, only to find a dark and demon-like creature looming over Lily's body, consuming her.

"No! Stop!" he shouted, watching the creature disappear with his wife. "No!"

"Heaven, wake up!"

"Huh?" Heaven popped his eyes open and found that he was no longer inside the bedroom. "What's happening?" He looked around and found himself back in the Golden City, Lily now levitating over the army of angels and turning into ashes and dust.

"Come on, we have to run!" Gabriel pulled Heaven onto a griffin and soared in the opposite direction.

"No! I can't! I have to save Lily!" Heaven pulled back.

But Gabriel was much too strong for him, and managed to lift him off his feet. "That's not Lily. It's Lilith!"

"That's impossible. I killed Lilith!"

Gabriel shook his head. "You thought you killed Lilith, but that was only a decoy. That's Lilith." He pointed to Lily, who was now targeting the cherubs. "We need to find a way to take her down. She's the portal, and as long as she's still alive, Lucifer will continue sending his army through. We need to shut off the source. Now!"

"But Lily! We'll kill her, too! I won't do it. I can't. I love her!"

Gabriel halted the griffin and turned to glare at him. "Do you want to turn into a pile of ashes? I sure don't! And I already told you, that's not Lily. That's pure evil. So, are you going to help me or not? Because I can't do this alone."

Heaven felt conflicted, but he knew there was only one right decision. "How do we kill her?"

"With this." Gabriel pulled out the Sword of a Thousand Warriors and handed it to Heaven. "Straight through the heart to close the portal."

"And what if it doesn't work? What if she sees me?"

"It will work, and don't worry. I'll distract her. But we need to act fast! God and the remaining angels can only bottleneck the portal for so long!"

Heaven nodded, gripping the sword in his hand as Gabriel charged toward Lily. He knew he was doing the right thing, but after all this time of trying to save her, he felt like he was betraying her. As they closed in on Lily, he saw the straining efforts of the angels, each one struggling to fight off the undead, and he knew he had to go through with it. He had to kill the woman he loved.

"Hey, ugly!" Gabriel shouted. "Over here!" He soared on his griffin in the opposite direction as Heaven flew toward the back of her heart. With one quick motion, he pierced the sword through her and leapt off.

A beam of darkness shot out from Lily's mouth and straight into the portal, sealing it off while the remaining undead army disintegrated.

Finally, peace was once again restored in the City of God. It was over.

Heaven felt a rush of déjà vu as he ran over to the fallen human. "I'm so sorry, Lily. I've failed you."

God walked over and placed a hand on Heaven's shoulder. "I'm proud of you, son. You saved our kingdom and our universe."

Heaven sniffed. "She's really gone, isn't she? It's not a spell anymore. There's no sacrificing my powers to save her. She's really gone."

"I'm afraid so," God replied.

Brushing the dirt off from her hair, Heaven held her body close, keeping her warm and safe even though he knew it was all over. The one creature he had tried so hard to protect. Gone. And there was no way to save her.

"But you are forgetting that I'm God."

Heaven looked up. "Father? You mean, you can save her?"

God nodded, and Heaven found himself back at the kitchen table in his home at Bodega Heights, placing the cold turkey sandwich in front of him.

After he took his first bite, he pulled the sheet of paper from his pocket and unfolded it.

"Please read," Heaven said, reading the words out loud. "You have served your kingdom well, a true hero. And because of that, Starwood now belongs to you. Lead it. Save the people before it turns into another Earth. I trust that you will do great things. God."

Suddenly, he heard a scream from their bedroom. Heaven dropped the note and rushed in, finding an ecstatic, and alive, Lily holding up her wedding ring.

"I've been looking for this for months! I was so scared that I had lost it! I can't imagine a life where I'm not married to you."

Heaven sat beside her on the bed and wrapped his arm around her shoulders. "Me, too, honey. Me, too."

HEAVEN ON EARTH

VIOLA TEMPEST

www.ingramcontent.com/pod-product-compliance
Lightning Source LLC
Chambersburg PA
CBHW031024190726
48286CB00003BA/1001